Heartstrings
MARILYN BOONE

Heartstrings
By Marilyn Boone

©2015 by Marilyn Boone

All rights reserved.
This book or parts thereof may not be reproduced in any form, stored in or introduced into a retrieval system, or transmitted, in any form, or by any means (electronic, mechanical, photocopying, recording, or otherwise) without prior written permission of the copyright owner and/or publisher of this book, except as provided by United States of America copyright law.

This book is a work of fiction. Names, characters, places, and incidents are a product of the author's imagination or are used fictitiously. Any resemblance to actual events, locales, or persons, living or dead, is coincidental.

Cover Design: Brandy Walker
www.sistersparrowgraphicdesigns.com
Interior Design: Jennifer McMurrain
www.lilybearhouse.com

ISBN-13: 978-1514166611
ISBN-10: 1514166615

Also available in eBook publication

PRINTED IN THE UNITED STATES OF AMERICA

This book is dedicated to cranes everywhere, who disguised as people…dance…

Prologue

*Tears traced a path down the woman's face as she
put her violin away
No longer would there be a song of freedom
Her son and her music were dead*

Budapest, Hungary, 1956…

Chapter One

Beads of perspiration trickled down Anna Holmes' forehead while she stood over the steaming containers of food, filling one plate after another. Only once did she stop long enough to wipe her face dry with the hem of her apron. It may have been the first day of autumn, but summer was refusing to give up its turn, transforming the kitchen at the Samaritan Center into a sauna instead.

"Hey, Miss Anna."

Anna looked up into the face that reminded her of soft, tanned leather and smiled. "Hi, Mr. Harmon, how is the new job going?"

"As long as it pays the bills and keeps Sugar happy then I'm happy," he chuckled.

Anna was puzzled by Mr. Harmon's answer. They had both been volunteering at the Samaritan Center for years now, and for some reason she assumed he lived alone. "I've never heard you talk about anyone named Sugar before."

Mr. Harmon flashed his warm but crooked grin. "Why, she's been my roommate ever since I heard her meowing at my door a few days ago. I didn't want her to be homeless like I once was."

Anna returned his grin despite the sting she felt when she heard the word homeless. "Sugar sounds like one lucky cat, but make sure you don't forget to take care of yourself first."

"Not to worry, Miss Anna. We take care of each other," he assured her with a long nod. "But look who's talking about taking care of yourself. You best take a break from that kitchen and cool off, or we'll soon be picking you up off the floor. Go on now, I'll take over."

Mr. Harmon was right. The heat was suffocating, and she wouldn't be of any help to anyone if she fainted. Leaving her apron on, Anna walked out the front door and found a small area against the building where there was an overhang of shade. She lifted her long auburn curls away from her neck then closed her eyes as a gentle breeze came to offer its small gift of relief.

"It looks like I came at the right time. Break time."

Anna's eyes flew open with a sudden rush of guilt for having left the kitchen. That was until she saw who was speaking to her.

"I'm E.C. Coleman, here to volunteer my services," he announced.

Anna already knew the name that went with the dark wavy hair and long eyelashes that never should have been wasted on a boy. She hesitated a moment then remembered the assignment their government teacher had made. Any student willing to participate in a community service project could earn extra credit. One of the choices he had listed was the Samaritan Center.

"You must be here to earn your bonus points," she said.

E. C. looked surprised. "Yeah, how did you know?"

Anna didn't take her eyes off of his while she answered, "Last hour government class, fourth row, sixth seat back."

"Sorry, I never noticed you were in there," he shrugged. "Isn't Mr. Jenkins great? All we have to do is show up, put in a few hours and we've got as good as an A."

Anna would never have expected E.C. Coleman to know she existed. He was on the football team and a member of the popular crowd. She wasn't. She was used to not being noticed. Even so, Anna wasn't about to let him think she was there only for a grade.

"I'm here every Wednesday afternoon and not because of any class. I need to get back to work now." She turned around to walk back inside, wishing he'd change his mind and go away.

E.C. followed behind her instead. "What is it I have to do?"

Anna wanted to tell him he didn't have to do anything, that the center didn't need his self-serving acts of charity. But it wasn't true. The number of volunteers had fallen over recent months, and they were in need of more help. "Sign in on the sheet by the door. I'll get you an apron and a pair of gloves."

E.C. put the apron on by himself, but was struggling to get the gloves stretched over his hands. "I can't get these things on. They're too small."

Anna was unmoved by his apparent frustration. "Sorry, they're one size fits all. Everyone has to wear them, it's the rules."

"In case you haven't noticed, my hands aren't like everyone else's," he spouted back.

She would have let him continue struggling on his own, but there were people waiting in line to be served, and she needed to relieve Mr. Harmon. "I'll help you this time."

Even after Anna discovered how much larger E.C.'s hands were, she was determined to make him wear them. "There, that wasn't so difficult," she finally said, basking in her private victory.

"Now, what?" he asked, still tugging at the gloves while walking with Anna to the food containers.

"Why don't you start by serving the green beans if you think you can handle it," she answered him.

E.C.'s only response was to pick up the large spoon and begin placing green beans onto the plates.

Anna stayed busy serving the mashed potatoes and meatloaf, but was able to catch an occasional glimpse of E.C. out of the corner of her eye. She didn't know much about him except that he was on the football team, and it was obvious how awkward he felt being there. His apron wasn't big enough to hide the stark contrast between his designer label clothes and those of the less fortunate they were handing meals to. Anna couldn't imagine he had any idea what it was like to need or want for anything.

"You could look up every once in a while and at least smile. Green beans can't be all that fascinating," Anna said after a while to break the silence between them.

"Excuse me. I didn't realize that was in the job description," E.C. replied coolly. "I thought I was just here to serve food."

Anna wished she had kept quiet. She turned away and fixed her eyes on the rows of tables filled with people eating what might be their only meal of the day. "I've been here long enough to learn that people are hungry for more than just food. Feeding their dignity is important, too."

"Well, since you seem to have had more practice at this, you can be their soul food while I take care of their stomachs," he said, ending with a smirk.

Anna started to tell him he had won the grand prize for being the rudest human being she had ever met, but then decided to save her breath. The people they were serving didn't fit into his privileged life style and neither did she. If E.C. Coleman knew about her past or where she lived, Anna was certain he would never speak to her again.

Relieved when it was time to stop serving, Anna's attention turned to removing the leftover food. That was until she heard the frenzied voice cry out from the dining room. "He's pointing at me again."

Anna didn't bother to offer E.C. an explanation. She ran from the kitchen to the table where a woman was on her feet, her eyes bulging with fear. Anna took the woman's hands and spoke gently. "It's all right Mrs. Harris, he's gone now. Go ahead and finish your dinner. I'll stay with you and make sure he doesn't come back."

A bewildered expression faded from the woman's face before she settled back in her chair and began eating again. Anna sat down in the empty chair next to her and glanced over at the serving window. E.C. was no longer in sight.

Once she was confident Mrs. Harris's delusion wouldn't return, Anna walked back into the kitchen where Mr. Harmon was stacking the dirty trays. "I guess the new volunteer already left?" she asked.

"Yes, ma'am, and he sure was in a hurry. As soon as I mentioned what an angel you were around here, he was gone in a flash," Mr. Harmon answered then shook his head. "You ought to have seen him getting those gloves off though."

Picturing E.C. battle the gloves for a second time made Anna laugh. She suspected he had already changed his mind about volunteering for extra credit. She wasn't at all surprised he was gone. She was more surprised by how long he stayed.

Anna grabbed a rag to wipe off the counters and wondered why Louisa hadn't joined them yet. She was usually in the kitchen by now, lathering and rinsing the dishes, while singing songs in a language no one at the center could understand. Anna worried that the housekeeping job had become too difficult for her, that the arthritis had gnarled her fingers too much. But

Louisa would be the last one not to do her work or complain.

Maybe she had fallen asleep while she was resting Anna thought, trying not to be alarmed. She finished the counters then looked down the hallway connecting the kitchen to Louisa's room and saw the door was closed. Anna considered knocking then changed her mind. There was no reason to disturb her. Louisa would come out when she was ready.

Anna went to the closet and pulled out her backpack and violin, being careful not to bump the case. Its frayed and cracked edges made it as worn and fragile as the instrument inside. "This was my great grandfather's," she had proudly announced the first time she took it to her orchestra class. But Anna didn't need to hear the snickering that followed to know how inferior her violin was compared to the others.

The words from her orchestra teacher still haunted her, "I believe you have a lot of talent, Anna. When you're able to get a better violin and take lessons, I know you'll be a fine player."

A few weeks later, Anna's father was laid off from his job and her younger brother had to be taken to the emergency room because of a severe asthma attack. Her parents had yet to be able to afford either one. If it hadn't been for Louisa, she would never have dreamed a music scholarship to the university was possible.

Anna stepped out of the Samaritan Center and thought back to the afternoon she first met Louisa. She had gone to the center early that Wednesday to practice her music, unaware that a new housekeeper had been hired. As she struggled through a difficult passage, a stranger's voice broke through her concentration.

"You must let the violin sing."

Anna's head jerked around to see an old woman with stooped shoulders and a head of disheveled white curls staring at her with piercing intensity.

"You must let the violin sing," the woman repeated.

Startled by this woman who seemed to have appeared out of nowhere, Anna stammered an apology. "I...I'm sorry. I don't have the best violin."

The woman looked tired and frail, but there was a determined spark in her eyes. "Every violin has a voice. You come here for a lesson this time every week, and I will help you to find it."

Anna had been too stunned to question the woman's peculiar accent or her knowledge of violins, much less what she was doing at the Samaritan Center. Curiosity drove her to arrive early again the next Wednesday where she found the woman sitting in a chair, waiting on her. Louisa had been teaching and guiding her ever since.

An unexpected swirl of cooler air wound around Anna's arms as she turned down the last block toward home. It produced a shiver as she held the handle to her violin case a little tighter. Maybe summer was going to let autumn have its chance after all. That's all Anna was hoping to have with her violin, just a chance.

Chapter Two

Anna fidgeted through most of her classes at school the next day, worried about going to her last hour. E.C. had probably already forgotten about her and the Samaritan Center by now, but she didn't want to do anything that might remind him. As long as she was already at her desk when he came in the room, he shouldn't notice her. He admitted that he never had before.

Anna's books were clutched in her arms and ready to go. As soon as the bell rang, she was out the door hurrying toward Mr. Jenkins' classroom. This time Anna chose a faster way even though it meant she would miss seeing her best friend, Jessie. She had to make sure she beat E.C.

"You're early today, Miss Holmes," Mr. Jenkins said, checking the time on the clock. "You must be excited to start our new unit on the Constitution."

Anna grinned. "How did you guess, Mr. Jenkins?"

Mr. Jenkins laughed and shook his head. He would always be one of her favorite teachers despite the less than pleasant experience his extra credit assignment had created for her. It wasn't his fault E.C. could be the poster boy for arrogance.

She attempted to start her algebra homework while waiting for class to begin, but her eyes kept shifting toward the door every time another student entered. The room was also getting louder with busy chatter about the upcoming football game against the Mustangs, Madison's biggest rival.

"Here's our number one quarterback," Mr. Jenkins announced.

Anna cringed at what sounded like the introduction of royalty and looked up from her paper just as E.C. walked in. Thankfully, he didn't even look in her direction.

"We're going to win tomorrow night, aren't we?" shouted a voice from the back of the room.

"Take a look at these hands," E.C. answered, holding them up. "They haven't failed me yet."

Anna knew those hands more intimately than she ever desired. He hadn't been quite as proud of them the day before when they were squeezed into tight rubber gloves. Maybe they possessed the skills necessary to win a football game, but she was unimpressed with how awkward they seemed when it came to holding a large spoon.

Mr. Jenkins waited until everyone was seated before he spoke again. "How many of you have decided to participate in the community service project?"

A few hands went up, but Anna thought none were as eager as E.C.'s.

"Would someone like to share their experience so far?" Mr. Jenkins probed further.

E.C. didn't hesitate. "It was easy. All I had to do was serve some green beans at the Samaritan Center. I even got to wear an apron," he joked, successful at getting some laughs.

Anna stiffened at his blatant shallowness. He would never understand what the Samaritan Center was about or the people that came there.

Mr. Jenkins seemed less amused as he targeted faces around the room. "No matter how simple the job may be, I hope all of you will come to know the importance of the service you're providing."

"Fat chance of that," Anna whispered under her breath, unaware she had added voice to her thoughts.

"Did you have something to add, Miss Holmes?" Mr. Jenkins asked.

Anna contained a gasp as she realized what she had done. "Yes…I mean, no."

"Why don't you ask her about the Samaritan Center, Mr. Jenkins? She was there." E.C. tossed Anna a glare brimming with challenge.

Anna felt the hair on the back of her neck rise, much like she witnessed when their old cat, Smoky, felt threatened. E.C. may have drawn his sword, but she refused to duel, keeping her eyes focused on Mr. Jenkins instead. She regretted ever informing E.C. they were in the same class. Nonexistence was preferable to humiliation.

Mr. Jenkins looked surprised. "I must have missed seeing your hand go up a minute ago."

Anna couldn't breathe while Mr. Jenkins held his gaze on her. It wasn't until he turned away that she released a quiet sigh of relief.

"As part of the assignment, I'm expecting you to write an essay describing your experience and what you learned from it. I wouldn't want extra credit to appear too easy to get," he said with a deliberate nod in E. C.'s direction.

Mr. Jenkins ignored the ripple of complaints throughout the room and continued, "Now, let's turn our attention to Article I of the Constitution and our legislative branch of government."

Anna was thankful Mr. Jenkins changed the topic, though she had a hard time staying focused for the rest of the hour. Requiring an essay would no doubt change some of her classmate's minds about earning extra credit. Maybe it would be enough to keep E.C. away from the Samaritan Center and her for good.

While Anna was anxious to find Jessie when class was over, she had an even greater desire to avoid further confrontation with E.C. She waited until she was at the end of the line of students to leave.

"Anna, may I speak with you for a moment?" Mr. Jenkins spoke up from his desk in the corner of the room.

The question caught Anna off guard causing her foot to catch on a chair as she turned around. She had nothing to be afraid of, but her heart's nervous pounding grew stronger the closer she got.

Mr. Jenkins smiled as she approached as if sensing her apprehension. By then she was the only student left in the classroom. "I just wanted to make sure there wasn't something said in class today that upset you. You didn't seem quite yourself."

Anna pressed her notebook close against her chest as if that would hide the inner turmoil she was feeling. "No, I'm fine."

"Is it true you are volunteering at the Samaritan Center with E.C.?" Mr. Jenkins continued.

"Yes," she answered. Anna wanted to tell him that it had nothing to do with his assignment, that she was already a volunteer. But then he might ask more questions, ones she wasn't ready to answer.

Mr. Jenkins studied her in a thoughtful manner before he spoke again. "Anna, you have the best grade in the class so you don't need the extra credit. I just wanted you to know I'm not going to require you to write an essay, though you can if you'd like. I'm proud of you for volunteering."

"Thank you." Anna was anxious for the conversation to be over before any more could be said. "Is that all you needed?"

Mr. Jenkins paused a moment then nodded.

"See you tomorrow." Anna spun herself around and left the room, determined never to let E. C. Coleman have this much control over her emotions again.

When a hand reached out and grabbed her elbow, Anna's whole body jerked away before she saw who it was. "Jessie!" She took another second to catch her breath. "Sorry, I didn't see you."

"That's obvious. A little jumpy are we?" Her best friend frowned. "First, I watched you almost trip in front of Mr. Jenkins and now this."

"I'm sorry. I wasn't expecting you to still be here. I figured you had already gone home," Anna apologized.

Jessie fell in step beside her. "My car is in the shop today. When you didn't show up at your locker I came to check on you so we could walk home together. What did Mr. Jenkins want with you anyway?"

Anna shrugged her shoulders. "He asked me about volunteering at the Samaritan Center."

"Did you tell him the real reason why you do it?" Jessie's eyebrows rose, waiting for an answer.

"No, and I don't intend to. Right now he thinks it's because of the extra credit assignment," Anna answered.

Jessie gave her a hard look. "You do a good thing, Anna."

"It doesn't seem like much considering all the meals they fed us after my father lost his job and we lost the house. Until we opened the café, we ate there almost every day. I feel like I owe them even more since I've been meeting Louisa there for violin lessons."

"How did your lesson go this week?" Jessie asked.

"Good...I think." Anna couldn't keep the hesitation from creeping into her voice.

Jessie's expression prompted her to explain further.

"She had forgotten it was Wednesday. Instead of waiting for me in the chair like usual, I found her in her room reading a book."

Jessie shrugged her shoulders. "We've all forgotten what day it was at one time or another."

"I suppose so," Anna agreed fighting back a persistent nudge of concern. "During my lesson she seemed her normal self, but then she was late coming to the kitchen to clean up. I didn't see her again before I left."

Quietness consumed their next steps until Jessie spoke again, "She is getting older, Anna. You've been lucky she's been around as long as she has."

Anna knew how lucky she was, though her orchestra teacher had yet to acknowledge how much she had improved. From the very first lesson, Louisa warned her against comparing herself to others, insisting that her time would come. If only Anna could believe she was right.

They had almost reached the corner where they separated ways when a nagging question slipped off Anna's tongue. "What's so special about a quarterback?"

Jessie's head drew back in surprise. "Since when did you take an interest in football?"

Anna instantly regretted asking. "Forget it...I was just curious that's all. I honestly don't care."

It was too late. Jessie's face brightened, lighting the amber hue of her eyes. "Come with me to the game tomorrow night so you can find out for yourself."

"I can't, I have to work at the café," Anna said, grasping for an easy excuse.

"Anna Holmes, you spend your whole life in that café or practicing your violin. We're seniors in high school and you've never been to a football game," Jessie reminded her. Her eyes then narrowed, "Remember our promise."

Jessie had played the trump card she knew Anna couldn't refuse. The pinky promise they made to each other when they were ten years old. Anna's shoulders dropped in defeat. "I suppose it won't hurt to go one time."

"You won't be sorry." Jessie walked away waving a triumphant good-by.

She already was, but there was something sacred in the simple promise that had bound their friendship for the past seven years.

Troubles shared,
Adventures dared,
Dragons slain,
Friends remain.

Anna took a deep breath as she resumed her walk alone. She would soon be experiencing her next dared adventure…a high school football game.

Chapter Three

By the time Anna got home from school the next day she was so tired of hearing about football, she wasn't sure how she was going to sit through an entire game. At least there had been a pep rally during her last hour so she didn't have to watch most of her government class swoon over E.C.'s very presence. And that included Mr. Jenkins.

She walked through the café and into the kitchen where she saw her mother standing at the counter chopping onions.

"Anna, an envelope came in the mail for you today. I took it up to your room and put it on your desk."

"Thanks, Mom." Anna started to go up the stairway that led to their bedrooms, but not before glancing at her mother again. There were bowls full of other vegetables waiting to be chopped or sliced. "Are you sure you don't need my help tonight? I really don't have to go to the football game."

Her mother smiled. "We'll manage just fine. You go ahead and have a fun evening."

Anna went to her room still not convinced, but anxious to see the envelope her mother was talking about. It was on her desk just as her mother had told her, though she had failed to mention that it was a large one. Anna set her books and violin down then hurried over to pick it up. The scripted logo on the front revealed right away it was from Truman, the local university. She held her breath a moment knowing it must be the scholarship application she had requested.

Opening the envelope, Anna pulled out the papers from inside and began reading the letter that had been included. *Dear Miss Holmes, We are pleased you are interested in attending Truman University and in auditioning to become a student in our nationally recognized music program...* The more Anna read the more nervous she became. This was it, the next big step toward making her dream a reality.

Anna finished looking over the application then realized how little time she had left to get ready before Jessie picked her up for the game. Despite her mother's words of assurance, Anna thought about feigning a sudden family emergency as an excuse for not going. But Jessie would see right through it and Anna would willfully have broken their oath, their promise of friendship. A best friend wouldn't do that.

Anna picked up a comb and pulled back the sides of her hair into a barrette, leaving a few loose tendrils to remain alongside her face. She even rummaged through a bag of seldom used eye shadow to find the right shade of pale green eye to complement the color of shirt she was wearing.

A final inspection gave Anna pause. Her naturally curly hair had a mind all its own and the few freckles sprinkled across her nose seemed like an afterthought of nature. An example of pretty would never include her, of that she was certain.

"I wish I could go to the game."

Anna's head swung away from the mirror to see her younger brother, Aaron, watching her from the doorway. She was surprised she hadn't heard him come up the stairs. Almost every one of the steps creaked. "It's just football. It can't be that big of a deal."

The longing projected from her eight-year old brother's eyes spoke otherwise. She felt sorry for him, knowing that football was his favorite sport and that he wasn't allowed to play outside much because of his asthma.

Anna walked over and lowered herself until she was at eye level in front of him, "What if I promise you the chance to meet Madison's quarterback? He's supposed to be volunteering at the center this Wednesday."

The words tumbled out of Anna's mouth before she thought about the consequences. She was only attempting to give her brother something to look forward to.

"You mean I could meet E.C. Coleman in person!" Aaron's stature grew taller with excitement.

Anna was happy with her brother's reaction, but it also surprised her. "How did you know his name?"

"Everybody knows who E.C. Coleman is," Aaron answered, unable to stand still any longer, "I've got to go tell Mom and Dad."

He ran from Anna's room leaving her alone to reflect on what had just taken place. She hadn't wanted E.C. to come back to the Samaritan Center, and now for Aaron's sake, she hoped he would. A sickening flow of worry pumped through every chamber of her heart. What if he wasn't willing to meet her brother or wasn't very nice to him if he did? As wrong as Anna thought it was, she didn't want E.C. shattering Aaron's heroic image of him. In her own way, she was as protective of her brother as their parents.

Anna heard a familiar honk from the street and ran to her window. "Be right down, Jessie."

She was hurrying through the kitchen when a question from her mother stopped her in mid-stride. "Anna, who is this football player your brother is suddenly talking about getting to meet?"

"Can I explain later, Mom? Jessie is waiting for me."

Her mother's eyebrows tilted in a paused thought before she waved her on. "All right, have a good time at the game."

Anna had to enter Jessie's blue Chevy through the back door then climb over the front seat to sit down. It was a ritual she had gotten used to, only this time she almost kicked Jessie in the head. "Are you ever going to get the handle fixed on this door?"

"It keeps life interesting, don't you think?" Jessie smiled at Anna before her whole expression changed.

"Why are you looking at me like that?" Anna leaned in to check herself in the rearview mirror. "Do I have too much makeup on?"

"No, there's nothing wrong," Jessie reassured her. "You just look different…in a good way," she was quick to add.

"It must be this fashionable new hairstyle." Anna placed her hand behind her head and jutted her chin upward. The pose made them both laugh, helping Anna forget about her dilemma with Aaron for at least a little while.

With the football stadium located so close to the cafe, it was only a matter of minutes until they had found a parking space and were out of the car. A sudden wave of anxiety kept Anna from following right behind Jessie. The stadium may as well have been a foreign country as awkward as she felt. She had never learned the language of high school, at first because her parents needed so much help getting the café opened, then later because it was simply easier not to.

"Come on," Jessie urged, "if you don't speed up, we're going to miss the kick-off." She bounced with anticipation as she ushered Anna faster toward the ticket booth. "I know you're going to love this."

Anna envied her best friend's perpetual enthusiasm. Orchestra class would be miserable without Jessie's comical faces from the cello section always trying to make her laugh. Jessie was convinced

Mrs. Carlson knew how good a violin player Anna was even though the hierarchy never changed. No matter how well Anna performed on her playing tests, Tonya Sterling would always sit first chair with her ally, Heather, beside her in second. It had been that way since seventh grade.

"Before I forget to tell you, guess what came in the mail today?" Anna quizzed Jessie while they waited in line.

Jessie looked at her with a frowned expression.

"The scholarship application..." Anna hinted.

Jessie's eyes suddenly widened, "From Truman?"

"Of course from Truman," Anna laughed at Jessie. "The auditions are being held in February. I just need to complete the application and have two letters of recommendation sent to the university by then."

"I'm sure Mrs. Carlson will write one for you, but will Louisa be able to write the other," Jessie started then hesitated, "...you know with her hands like they are?"

Anna pictured Louisa's crippled hands and knew it wouldn't be easy for her. "I think so," she answered with more optimism than she felt, especially in her present surroundings.

"Don't worry. Once the judges hear you play, they'll be so awestruck by your talent, nothing else will matter," Jessie's dramatic proclamation ended with both her hands pressed over her heart.

Anna shook her head and smiled, wishing she had half of Jessie's confidence. Then noticing they were next in line, she opened her purse to get her billfold.

Jessie grabbed Anna's hand before she had the chance. "No you don't. This game's on me."

Anna started to protest but knew it wouldn't do any good. Once Jessie's mind was made up there was no changing it. With their tickets in hand, Jessie sped through the gate and began weaving her way through the crowd. Anna had never had to excuse herself so many times before. The national anthem had just finished playing, and it was all Anna could do to keep up with her, much less battle the gnawing feeling that being there was a huge mistake.

They squeezed into a space in front of the band as the teams lined up for the kick-off. Drum rolls led the cheers as the football was launched down the field to the opposing team. A blitz of Madison's black and gold uniforms immediately followed ready to make the tackle.

"The poor guy that caught the ball didn't have a chance," Anna said, sitting down after the play.

"This is supposed to be the best team Madison has had in twenty years, thanks to our awesome quarterback, E.C. Coleman," Jessie shot back.

Jessie's description made Anna's eyes roll. No wonder he had such an inflated ego if that's how everyone talked about him. She knew she should tell Jessie about meeting him at the Samaritan Center, but this didn't seem like the right time or place.

"Hey, we have the ball now, and there's the quarterback. He's number 12," Jessie pointed out to Anna.

Anna didn't need Jessie to remind her which player wore that number. The stadium echoed with voices chanting, "Let's go, E.C., let's go." She watched as he stepped back and threw the football to one of his receivers who ran for several yards before being forced out of bounds. In what seemed like an identical play, the receiver again caught the ball then ran across the goal line, giving Madison High their first touchdown.

The crowd jumped to their feet as the band played the school's fight song. Despite her initial hesitation, Anna was quickly swept into the excitement. To her astonishment, she began cheering as loudly as Jessie.

By the end of the first half the score was 21 to 7 in Madison's favor, and Anna realized how much the cheering had made her thirsty.

"I need something to drink, how about you?" Jessie asked as if she had read Anna's mind.

"Yeah, let's go," Anna grabbed her purse and started to stand up.

Jessie stopped her. "Why don't you stay here and save our places? It'll be faster if I go by myself."

Jessie was off before Anna had a chance to respond. She wasn't as comfortable sitting by herself, but Jessie was probably right. It would be faster without her tagging along.

Anna inhaled a deep breath of the cool night air and dared to look around. The bright lights, the scoreboard, and all the markings on the field were easier to study now.

"Hey, aren't you in my algebra class?"

Anna twisted around just far enough to see that the question came from a boy at the end of their bleacher. He was looking straight at her, leaving no doubt the question was meant for her.

A warm tingle in Anna's cheeks warned her that a blush was in the making. "Yes, I think so," she answered, wishing she could make herself invisible.

"It's good to see you at the game," he said before turning back to his group of friends.

It was a curse to become embarrassed so easily. Anna was thankful she hadn't reacted in the same way when E.C. showed up at the Samaritan Center. Maybe it was because the center was her territory. This football stadium wasn't.

Anna concentrated on watching the band march into different formation during their halftime show until she spotted the Jessie's head of short dark hair bouncing up the steps toward her.

"Why is your face red?" Jessie asked, handing Anna a large cup and settling back into place.

Anna tilted her head and eyes in the direction of the boy at the end of the bleachers.

Jessie poked her with her elbow. "He's kind of cute. Did he say something to you?"

"A little," Anna shrugged.

"We're going to have to get you over these blushing episodes," Jessie said with sudden determination. "Why shouldn't a boy want to talk to you? You're no ugly duckling, you know."

Anna was quick to dismiss Jessie's evaluation. She knew that was only a best friend's opinion. But

Jessie was right about the blushing episodes. They had become a nuisance every time a boy looked her way.

The second half started with another easy touchdown for Madison, followed by two more. From what Anna could gather, all the quarterback had to do was step back and decide whom to throw the ball to.

"Look at E.C., the game is almost over and he's hardly even dirty," Anna leaned over and whispered to Jessie.

"Only because he has some good blocking to protect him," Jessie said.

Anna was about to tell Jessie that E.C. didn't seem to need protection from anything when gasps from the crowd drew their attention to the middle of the field. They had missed the play but watched with intense curiosity as a large tackle unfolded, leaving one of Madison's black and gold players on the ground.

The stadium had grown too quiet for Anna to feel comfortable asking Jessie who it was, so she tried to read the number on the jersey herself. It wasn't until the coaching staff helped the injured player to his feet that everyone could see the number 12 and began applauding. By the way he walked it was apparent E.C.'s legs weren't hurt, but his left arm was cradled against him as he approached the sidelines.

Jessie pointed to the clock on the scoreboard. "It's a good thing there's only two minutes left in the game and we're winning."

"It's even better that it isn't his right arm that's hurt," Anna added.

Jessie turned to look at her. "You didn't notice? He's left-handed."

Anna sat quietly. No, she hadn't noticed. But then she pictured them serving together at the Samaritan Center. That may have been one of the reasons he looked so awkward when he was serving the green beans. He had been holding the spoon in his right hand.

The tone in the stands turned grave as fans could be heard murmuring their concerns over E.C's unknown fate. If the injury was serious, what would that mean for the team and for the season? For Anna, what would that mean for Aaron?

She had a difficult time watching the remainder of the game after the substitute quarterback was put in. Her eyes kept glancing to the bench where E.C. was resting with an ice pack covering his arm. Whatever his injury was, it didn't look like he would be volunteering again at the Samaritan Center. Her thoughts were bittersweet, knowing how disappointed Aaron was going to be not to meet him.

"10…9…8…7." Anna heard Jessie begin counting down and joined in for the last few seconds.

Jessie then pulled on her arm. "Let's see if we can beat this crowd out of here."

Anna tried to catch a final glimpse of the team on their way to the locker room but people were already down on the field swarming around them.

"Admit I was right. You loved going didn't you?" Jessie said once they were farther away from the noise.

Anna couldn't deny that going to the game changed something inside her. Until a few days ago her feelings were straightforward and predictable. Now, they no longer seemed in her control. A boy she had just met and immediately disliked, she found herself feeling sorry for.

"All right, I admit it was fun," Anna managed a grin. "At least I now know what a quarterback does."

She decided to postpone telling Jessie about E.C. since she would probably never be talking to him again anyway. Instead, Anna looked toward home and was reminded of how much Aaron wanted to be there. Her new promise would be to take him to the next home game. That was a promise Anna was determined to keep.

Chapter Four

Anna's hand pounded the nightstand until she found the right button to silence her alarm clock. Quiet once again, she sunk into the comfort of her blankets, needing just a few more minutes to separate her dream thoughts from her wakening reality.

But Anna already knew what the reality was. It was Wednesday again, the day she told Aaron he could meet E.C. at the Samaritan Center. E.C. was lucky to have only suffered a sprained wrist in the game, but he was still wearing a splint. Between his injury and the required essay, Anna was confident he wouldn't be volunteering there any longer.

"Aren't you going to school today?"

Anna's eyes snapped open at the sound of her brother's voice before raising her head to look at the time. "I must have gone back to sleep."

"Well you better get up, 'cause today's the day I get to meet E.C. Coleman," Aaron continued, looking as if he could explode with anticipation.

Anna sat up reluctant to leave the nest of warmth but even more so, because she felt responsible for the disappointment she knew was coming for her brother. "Aaron, I don't think E.C. will be at the center today."

"But you promised, and I've already told my friends," he responded in a pitch bordering on desperation.

Anna forced herself out of bed and hurried toward her dresser. "I'm sorry, Aaron, but you'll just have to explain to your friends that he's still injured and couldn't come. I'm sure they'll understand," she said while yanking open one drawer after another.

In the next glance, Anna saw her brother drop his head and turn to leave. "Aaron, wait a minute. I know it's not the same as meeting E.C. in person, but how about I take you and one of your friends to the next game? I think I've almost talked Mom and Dad into it."

Anna watched his face brighten a little before he ran off, making her feel only slightly better. As soon as she had her parents' approval, she would only have Jessie left to convince that taking two eight-year-old boys to a football game was a dream come true.

She went to her closet and finally settled on a burgundy sweater not too different from the shade of her hair. "No beauty awards today," she grunted as she stopped in front of the mirror to comb her hair into a quick ponytail. Then grabbing one of the recommendation forms from Truman, Anna ran down the stairs.

Bye, Mom," Anna said, cutting through the kitchen where her mother was already busy rolling out the pastry for the day's pies.

"Have a good day," her mother said before bringing her hands to an abrupt stop. "Oh, Anna, do you know anything about this E.C. Coleman your brother is talking about? I was just wondering if Charlie Coleman was his father."

Anna tried to answer without slowing down. "I have no idea, Mom. All I know is if I don't hurry, I'm going to be late to first hour."

She carefully maneuvered her way out the door while holding onto her violin case and books. This had to be one of the worst beginnings to a morning, ever. Of all the days to oversleep, ruin one of her brother's most anticipated moments in his short life, miss breakfast, and have her mother mention another Coleman name. Today, her attention needed to stay focused on her playing test in orchestra. She didn't want to let herself down, but more especially, she didn't want to let Louisa down.

Anna usually walked to school down Winston Drive. It was her favorite street, lined on both sides with some of the largest and oldest homes in town. The one she loved the most was known as the Baxter mansion. Its tall wrought iron fence surrounding the estate and arched wooden front door reminded her of a medieval castle. Anna thought it would be a perfect home for a princess if ever one was to live in Madison.

The home had been built by the founder of Baxter Industries, the company her father worked for until he was laid off from his job. Anna didn't know who lived there now. She never saw anyone going in or coming out and decided she preferred to keep it that way, as a place of mystery and intrigue, maybe even secrets.

But there was no time for fairy tales this morning. Walking down Winston Drive would take too long. Anna had no choice but to take the faster route through town if she was to have any chance of getting to school on time. She picked up her pace, frustrated when the light turned red before she could cross Main Street.

"Hey baby, need a ride?" a voice hollered out.

The words slithered into Anna's hearing as if under the power of an experienced snake charmer. In her peripheral vision she saw a boy leaning out the window of a car that had pulled up to the stoplight beside her. She fought the instinct to turn her head, hoping the offer was intended for someone else close by.

He continued with a slow whistle. "Nice sweater…almost matches your hair."

If Anna had made her face more visible, he would have seen another shade of red added to her palette of color. There was no doubt she was the object of his unwelcome attention.

"Leave her alone, Taylor," a different and deeper voice cut in, though it was barely audible above the loud music playing from the radio.

"I'm just obliged to be friendly," he said, trying to justify himself.

Anna kept her eyes focused on the light, trying to stare it into turn green. Once it finally did, she was able to get a better view of the car as it drove past. She had no idea what kind it was, but it was dark blue with a style that screamed new and expensive.

Crossing the street, Anna's mind raced as fast as her body, trying to remember where she had recently heard the name Taylor. And then it came. The announcer at the football game kept repeating over the loud speaker that the ball had been passed to a Madison football player with that same name. A sudden realization that E.C. could have been the driver of the car produced an unexpected shiver.

Anna forced the possibility aside, needing to concentrate instead on not being late to school. As soon as the building was in sight, she saw students running down the sidewalk toward the entrance and knew she had only seconds to spare. She sped up as best she could while carrying her violin, not stopping until she reached the door outside of her classroom.

While taking a moment to catch her breath, Anna spied Jessie motioning to her from her desk in the classroom across the hall. She gave up trying to figure out what Jessie was trying to communicate, and slipped into her seat just as the final bell stopped ringing. Anna breathed in a sigh of relief as the morning's frantic grip gradually began to let go.

That's when the question her mother asked her came to mind. Anna had never heard of Charlie Coleman and was a little curious why it seemed to matter to her mother that E.C. might be his son. The name Charlie did begin with the letter C and the C, in E.C. had to stand for something. She then shook the thought away. There were probably several people named Coleman in this town and they couldn't all be related.

Anna spent the rest of the morning trying to quiet her stomach's persistent protests of hunger and was glad when it was time for lunch. She walked out the main door to the school and took the note out of her pocket that Jessie had handed her after first hour. *Meet me on the front steps at 11:45,* Anna read again. It was almost noon now.

"All right, Jessie. Where are you?" Anna mumbled to herself as she sat down on the top step to continue waiting. They weren't going to have time to drive anywhere to eat if she didn't hurry.

A cool breeze wove through the sun's rays making Anna glad she had chosen a sweater to wear despite the comment it invited that morning. Growing impatient, her left hand practiced the motions of a difficult fingering pattern she would be playing on her violin the next hour.

Anna stopped when the doors opened behind her and a group of people came walking out. She turned to see if Jessie was among them and came face to face with E.C. instead. Their eyes drew together like magnets before their heads quickly spun away from each other.

E.C. and his friends were down the steps and cutting across the grass when one of the voices she heard was sickeningly familiar. It sounded just like the one that called out to her at the stoplight. Anna dared to glance in their direction to see if she could identify who the voice belonged to.

"Sorry I took so long." Jessie seemed to have come from nowhere and was out of breath as she sat down next to Anna. "I had to go back to my locker to get these."

Anna took the brown paper sack Jessie was holding out for her, but her attention was still on E.C. Coleman and his group as they continued to walk toward the parking lot. "Jessie, do you know who that short boy is with E.C.?" she whispered, even though they were a far enough distance away by then not to hear.

Jessie followed Anna's line of vision. "You mean 'Tidbit'?" She gave a look of disgust before adding, "He's in my history class."

"Tidbit?" Anna covered her mouth to keep a burst of laughter from erupting.

"Of course that's just a nickname," Jessie said, joining in Anna's amusement. "His real name is Taylor Gibbs, and he has a very inflated opinion of himself."

He's in perfect company with E.C. then, Anna thought. "I think he tried to flirt with me this morning while I was walking to school."

"That doesn't surprise me. He thinks he's heaven's gift to the entire female population." Jessie paused a moment. "But as annoying as he is, at least he's good for one thing."

"And that is…," Anna prompted.

"He's the best receiver on the football team…you know the one that catches the football and runs to get a touchdown," Jessie teased her before looking in the direction of the street.

Anna watched as the same dark blue car that had pulled up beside her that morning was driving in front of the school with its passenger, Taylor Gibbs, in plain view.

"Look at that beautiful new Camaro," Jessie said, her voice dripping with envy. "E.C. must be one proud owner."

Anna shrugged her shoulders, he was proud all right. So what if it had been him at the stoplight. So what if he drove an expensive sports car. Nothing about E.C. Coleman was going to matter except where her brother was concerned.

"That's enough about them, let's start eating." Jessie pulled a sandwich out of her sack and started to unwrap it. "My famous ham and cheese sandwich with no mustard, just like you like them."

Anna took out her sandwich as well. "Thanks, Jessie. At least my stomach will be happy during the playing test." She was afraid their conversation had made her lose her appetite, but once she took a bite, she didn't stop until she was finished.

She then looked at Jessie, trying hard to be serious, "By the way, I have a proposition for you."

"Am I going to like it?" Jessie asked, squinting back at her.

Anna's eyebrows lifted with the smile she was unable to contain any longer. "How about going on a double date with me to the game Friday night?"

Jessie looked confused at first, and then returned the smile. "Does he come above my waist?"

"A little," Anna said, forming a hopeful expression as she waited for Jessie's answer.

"Why not, I'm sure it will be better than some of the real dates I've been on," she said, causing them both to laugh out loud.

Anna knew her best friend wouldn't let her down. The only question now was if Anna would be able to do the same for Aaron.

Chapter Five

All the memories from Anna's unpleasant morning vanished as soon as her playing test was over and she saw the surprised look on Mrs. Carlson's face. For a moment, her orchestra teacher appeared to be at a loss for words until she finally nodded and said, "Very nice work, Anna."

Anna stood up to leave thinking she was finished, but Mrs. Carlson stopped her. "Anna I'd like you to audition for the All-District orchestra. You're already familiar with most of the music. It would just require a little extra practice."

When she didn't get a response right away, Mrs. Carlson continued with words that spoke directly to Anna's insecurities, "To be one of the best, Anna, you have to compete with the best. You can think about it and let me know tomorrow if you'd like."

The immediate temptation was to tell Mrs. Carlson she couldn't possibly be ready in time, that she wasn't good enough. But this time Anna's conscience fought back, not allowing her fears to be an excuse like they had before. Even if she didn't make it, the experience would be good practice for her audition with Truman.

Anna knew to answer quickly before she changed her mind. "No, I'll do it."

Once school was out, Anna hurried to get to the Samaritan Center. There was so much to talk to Louisa about, the recommendation form from Truman she had tucked inside her music folder and now an audition for the All-District orchestra.

"Louisa!" Anna called out as she set her books and violin down on the table and glanced around the room. She was nowhere to be seen. Anna tried not to be concerned, but this was the second Wednesday in a row Louisa hadn't been sitting in a chair waiting for her. Then Anna heard a crash.

Running toward the sound, she found Louisa kneeling on the kitchen floor next to a pan of spilled water. Anna rushed to her side. "Are you all right?"

Louisa shook her head, looking humiliated by the puddle that surrounded their shoes. "I feel so clumsy."

"It's all right, it's only water. Yesterday, a bowl of soup slipped right out of my hands at the café. Everywhere I stepped there was a chopped vegetable," Anna said with a light chuckle, hoping to minimize Louisa's self-reproach. "I'll help you clean it up."

Anna went to the drawer and pulled out a couple of dishtowels. It wasn't until she turned back around that she got a thorough look at Louisa's appearance. First, she noticed the pink plastic curlers on Louisa's head, precariously attached by thin strands of her white hair. Then Anna's eyes moved to the green satin blouse and long black skirt, both of which looked like they hadn't seen the light of day in years.

Feelings of apprehension grew inside Anna. She had never seen Louisa in anything but navy blue stretch pants paired with only a handful of different shirts. To her knowledge, Louisa never had visitors or went anywhere in which she needed to dress up. "Are you going somewhere?"

Louisa's eyes sparkled with an answer that seemed to emanate from deep within her. "No, Felix is coming here. I'm so happy you will get to meet him."

The words had a disturbing ring to them as Anna's mind sought to recall her ever speaking about anyone with that name. "If you need to finish getting ready, I don't have to have a violin lesson today."

Louisa's expression changed to one of alarming resolve. "Oh, but you must have your lesson. There will be plenty of time before Felix arrives."

Anna continued to study Louisa. Whoever Felix was, he wouldn't want to see her looking like this. "Why don't you at least let me help you fix your hair? That way you'll have one less thing to worry about while getting ready."

Louisa smiled and nodded her agreement.

"Then Anna's Beauty Salon is now at your service," she said with a bow, relieved to hear her teacher and friend respond with her familiar laugh.

Louisa led the way into her room and sat down at a desk that had a small mirror hanging on the wall above it. Anna removed the curlers, being careful not to tangle them. As she began combing through the wiry strands of hair, she imagined the stories they could tell her about Louisa's life.

Anna had always refrained from asking Louisa about her past; afraid the questions might upset her and make her disappear as unexpectedly as she had appeared. But she often wondered how Louisa knew so much about playing the violin. She spoke with such authority during her lessons and guided Anna through the music without ever touching her instrument. Everything she had taught her so far was correct. In fact, Anna had a strong suspicion that somehow Louisa knew more about playing the violin than Mrs. Carlson.

"Felix must be someone special," Anna said unable to resist the temptation to find out more about the person who seemed to be of such importance to Louisa.

"Oh, he is," she answered, first proud then pensive. "I haven't seen him for so long, ever since the uprising."

A cloud of uneasiness filled the space between them. Before Anna dared to respond, Louisa continued, "I begged him not to go. Our Hungary was no match against their strong soldiers, but Felix wouldn't listen. He was my only son…." her voice trailed off.

Anna was stunned. If Louisa came from Hungary then the accent and foreign songs she sang made sense. But having a son who died? She was afraid Louisa was being preyed upon by some terrible memory or even worse, that she was starting to hallucinate.

Forcing her worries aside, Anna finished Louisa's hair and stepped back to examine the results. "There, that looks better."

Anna was laying the comb back on the desk when Louisa grabbed hold of her arm. Despite their covering of fragile skin and their gnarled form, Louisa's hands possessed a determined strength that could still be felt.

"Thank you," Louisa said, looking into the mirror directly at Anna.

"You're welcome," Anna replied, returning her gaze, unable to decipher the additional message she felt radiating from Louisa's eyes.

"Now, it is time for your lesson." Louisa stood up with purpose and turned to walk out of the room.

Anna followed right behind her, eager to get back to her normal Wednesday routine. She hesitated a moment before taking her violin out of its case. "Mrs. Carlson asked me today if I would audition for the All-District orchestra. Do you believe I should?"

"What do you believe?" Louisa asked, returning into the serious teacher she became during her lesson.

Anna knew the answer that Louisa expected, yet her insecurities were always ready to extinguish any confidence she had gained in herself. "I have just as good a chance as anyone else if I work hard enough," she answered, using the same words Louisa had spoken to her over and over during the past two years.

"Three things you must never forget, form, focus, and then freedom. You must give your music wings, for that is how it travels into the hearts of those who hear it." Louisa pointed a finger as she added, "Of course, you should audition."

Anna picked up her music folder. "The scholarship application from Truman also came in the mail. I brought one of the recommendation forms for you to fill out whenever you have the chance."

New doubts began to surface as Anna placed the form on the table. She couldn't help but worry about Louisa's mental state now in addition to her ability to use her hands to write.

Concentrating on her music during her lesson was difficult with Louisa's odd choice of clothes in constant view. Not to mention the new questions that kept drumming in her mind. Did Louisa really have a son named Felix? And if so, then what happened to her husband?

After the lesson was over, Louisa took the form from the table and went back to her room. Nothing more was mentioned again about Hungary or Felix. The window to Louisa's past that had opened ever so slightly had been shut again.

Anna put her violin and books away and started getting the plates and trays ready for the serving line. She went through the motions feeling completely detached from the activity going on around her. Even the aroma that permeated the air was too familiar a smell to penetrate her thoughts and concerns about Louisa.

"Miss Anna, are you with us?"

Anna glanced up to see Mr. Harmon give her a wink. "Of course I'm here Mr. Harmon. Where else would I be on Wednesday?" she teased him with a smile.

"I was just checking 'cause that's the second time I've called your name. I saw that your body was here, but the rest of you looked to be a million miles away. That friend of yours is going to be showing up soon and you might not even know it," Mr. Harmon answered.

Anna winced at the insinuation that she and E.C. were friends. Nothing could be farther from the truth. "Mr. Harmon, that boy is not my friend. He was only volunteering here so he could earn some bonus points for a class at school. Between what happened with Mrs. Harris last week and the injury he got in the football game, I'll bet you a penny he won't be here today," she said with a decided certainty while pulling out the silverware container.

"Well," Mr. Harmon chuckled then paused, "today must be my lucky day then. It looks like I'm one copper richer."

Anna joined Mr. Harmon's gaze in looking toward the entrance to the center. E.C. was walking straight toward them. This time there was something unsettling about his assured and indifferent manner, and she didn't like it. Her nervousness heightened the closer he came making her wish she was wearing a coat of armor to protect herself.

E.C. reached her before she could compose what to say to him. "Where do you want me to start?" he asked.

Anna's eyes fell to his hand. The splint was gone but it was still taped. "I'm surprised you came today," she said, not intending to ignore his question.

E.C. lifted his hand. "One little injury like this won't keep me from doing what I want to do, though getting those gloves on might be a problem."

She couldn't imagine that he truly wanted to be there, especially after his quick escape the week before. Holding back the stinging response that rushed to the tip of her tongue, Anna thought about her brother. She already told him E.C. wouldn't be there and made a deal to take him to the football game instead. But how could she deny Aaron the chance to get what he really hoped for. All she would have to do is ask E.C. if he would stay a few minutes longer.

"Don't worry about the gloves. Maybe it would be easier for you to pour drinks today anyway." Anna did her best to sound friendly. She directed E.C. toward the pitchers of water and tea, and then began filling the trays herself.

An hour passed by before Anna's job slowed down enough for her to calm her nerves and find the courage to ask E.C. about meeting Aaron. A couple of times she felt he was watching her, either out of pity or sheer boredom she guessed. Anna hardly took her eyes off the people in line and only once had to ask for more tea to be poured. She was grateful there hadn't been any disturbances. Even Mrs. Harris seemed preoccupied with happier, non-delusional thoughts.

Anna cleared her throat and looked at E.C.. The time was now or never. "Are you in a hurry to get somewhere after you leave here?"

E.C. threw his head back slightly. "Not usually."

"Would you mind waiting around for a few extra minutes today?" she asked, unsure how to read the perplexity spreading across his face.

"Do you need a ride home or something?"

"No." Anna cringed inside at the abruptness in her voice. This conversation wasn't heading in any direction she wanted to go.

"What I'm trying to say is I have a little brother who loves football, and I was wondering if you wouldn't mind if he came up to meet you," she seemed to blurt out all at once.

E.C. lifted his shoulders. "Sure."

Anna didn't want to give him the chance to change his mind. "I'll be right back," she said and left the kitchen to get to the telephone in the small office.

All she had to do was mention to her mother that the football player she wondered might be Charlie Coleman's son was at the Samaritan Center for Aaron to meet. Her mother offered to bring her brother there right away.

Anna returned to the kitchen and couldn't believe what she saw. A few latecomers were lined up at the serving window with E.C. filling the plates the best he could.

"He'll be here in a few minutes," she said, hurrying to take over for him. "Thanks."

"No problem," he answered matter-of-factly.

Anna finished handing out what she hoped would be the last tray. "It will mean a lot to Aaron."

E.C.'s head snapped around. "What did you say his name was?"

The intensity of his tone took Anna by surprise. Their conversation had been going better than she expected up until now. She looked at E.C. and repeated, "Aaron."

She could see the muscles in his jaw ripple with movement while his eyes were fixed on hers. Anna grappled to figure out what she did or said that would cause this kind of reaction from him. What if he all of a sudden left like he had the week before? She tried to keep her worry at bay by carrying the empty food containers to the sink. Louisa should be appearing soon to wash them as long as she hadn't fallen asleep again.

"Anna!"

Anna turned toward the sound of her brother's voice and couldn't help but return his big smile.

Aaron tugged on her sleeve, and she bent down for him to whisper in her ear. "Is that him over by the drinks?"

She nodded her head and was ready to take him over to introduce him to E.C. when Aaron ran off without her.

By the time she walked over to them they were already shaking hands. The change she had witnessed in E.C.'s demeanor was gone, and Aaron's face was beaming. Anna found herself envious of his excitement.

"Did you really recover a fumble and run the ball in for a touchdown once?" Aaron asked.

E.C. laughed. "That was during the final play of the season last year."

"No wonder you're a hero," Aaron said, his eyes opening wider with awe.

Anna observed how easy their conversation was and remained silent until now. "It's just a game of football, Aaron."

"But you got to go to the game last week, and I heard you telling Mom how much you liked it," he defended himself.

Aaron's honesty made Anna warm with discomfort. That wasn't information she wanted him to share in front of E.C..

For the first time in this three-way conversation, E.C. looked at her. "I didn't figure you were the type to like football."

"I don't, I was just doing a friend a favor," she answered, employing her stubborn pride to redeem herself.

"Don't forget your promise to take me and Jeffery to the game Friday," Aaron reminded her.

Anna was growing impatient to put an end to this meeting. "I'm sure you won't let me."

As if Louisa read her mind and was coming to her rescue, she entered the kitchen singing the same song she always sang on Wednesdays. Anna couldn't understand any of the words but she had heard it enough times to have the tune memorized. It was a huge relief for her to see that Louisa had also changed back into her normal clothes.

Louisa looked surprised to see them standing by the serving counter. "What brings you here today, Master Aaron?"

Though Anna knew Louisa was just teasing Aaron, the title wasn't that far from the truth. For the past few years his asthma had dictated almost everything the family could or couldn't do.

"I got to meet the quarterback of the football team," he answered with a grin that showed the spaces of his two lost teeth.

At least he didn't mention the word hero thought Anna before she recognized that it was her cue to introduce them to each other.

"Louisa, this is E.C. Coleman, he's volunteering here for a class assignment. E.C. this is Louisa..." Anna faltered slightly, unprepared to say a last name she forgot she didn't know. What else could she say about Louisa? That she lived in a small room at the Samaritan Center, that she was the housekeeper there, that she was her violin teacher. None of them sounded dignified enough or believable.

They acknowledged each other with a slight bow of the head then Louisa continued with her singing as she took her place at the sink.

"So, do you want to play football someday?" E.C. asked Aaron.

Aaron hung his head. "I doubt if my parents will ever let me."

"How about for now, you meet me up here on Wednesdays and we'll play catch for a few minutes after I'm finished. That is, if it's okay with your mom and dad, and of course, your sister." E.C. directed his last words at Anna.

Anna knew she should be glad that E.C. was granting her brother so much attention but this was far more than she expected or wanted. Looking at Aaron's hopeful face, however, she knew she couldn't refuse his offer. "It should be all right."

"Yes!" Aaron swung a fist in front of him before raising his hand to give E.C. a high five.

"See you next week then." E.C. was leaving the kitchen when he stopped to speak to Louisa, "It was nice to meet you, ma'am."

Anna was astonished. E.C. had been nothing but charm and manners when it came to meeting her brother and Louisa. She couldn't help but be skeptical of his sincerity.

"He seems like a pleasant young man," Louisa commented after he was gone.

Anna stared blankly at her. She could understand the innocent judgment coming from an eight-year old, but not Louisa. Whatever kind of spell Louisa had fallen under, she was bound to change her mind once she witnessed what E.C. was really like.

"We'll know soon enough," was all the charity Anna was willing to give him.

Chapter Six

Anna brought her audition pieces for All-District to her lesson the next week and watched as Louisa looked them over.

"This one, *The Moldau*," Louisa said, tapping her finger against the music. "What do you know about it?" She stood firm, waiting for an answer.

"I believe Mrs. Carlson said it was the name of a river." Anna was almost positive that's what she had heard, though Mrs. Carlson rarely talked about the music or its composers.

"That is correct, but it's not just any river. It flows for three hundred miles throughout the countryside and villages of Czechoslovakia. This music is the story of its journey." Louisa paused then spoke again, "I want you to close your eyes."

Louisa's request was puzzling, but Anna did what she was told.

"Now play the first line without opening them."

Anna positioned her violin underneath her chin and placed her bow on the strings. "I don't have the notes memorized."

Louisa was undeterred. "Your fingers will remember them. Now, I want you to make me hear a river."

The first few measures were awkward, but Anna kept playing until she could feel the rhythm in the phrasing. Her mind began to picture a small trickling stream, merging and growing until it became a large winding river. Anna was surprised when her bowing came to a stop and she realized she had not only played the first line, but the first page.

By the end of her lesson, Anna's arms were as weary as if they had actually played for three hundred miles. They trembled as she set her violin down and sought to understand what drove Louisa's urgency to have her work so hard. Anna could only figure she must have felt the need to push her harder because of the recommendation form from Truman as well as the upcoming audition for All-District.

Closing the latch on her violin case, she wondered how much longer it would last before the case broke beyond repair. That it had held together for this many years was a miracle to her. She walked into the kitchen and placed her violin in the cabinet, releasing a weary sigh.

"Do you play?"

Anna spun around to see E.C. propped against the doorway looking at her. She was so startled by his voice, she was thankful the violin was no longer in her hands. Otherwise, she may have dropped it.

"Play what?" Anna presumed not to know what he was asking about.

"That was a violin you just put away, wasn't it?" he said, raising an eyebrow.

"Oh, that," she answered trying to make his observation seem insignificant. "I just play it in the school orchestra."

Anna didn't feel the need to elaborate. A star football player probably wouldn't be the type to care much about music, at least not that kind. She picked her books up off the counter to put on the shelf above, careful not to let her face give away how heavy they felt.

"Then you must know Tonya Sterling. She plays in the orchestra," E.C. continued.

"I know who she is," Anna hesitated, biting back the "unfortunately" that threatened to follow. She had long ago accepted that Tonya Sterling was one of Mrs. Carlson's favorite students and would always sit in first chair. What bothered her more was how much Tonya took her position for granted, not to mention the total lack of appreciation she showed for her much nicer violin.

Anna was too tired to feel like talking much, especially about someone like Tonya, the school's unofficial queen of snobs. "Aren't you here awfully early?

"Coach gave us a shorter practice today so I thought I'd come on over and see if there was anything extra I could do to help."

Anna had to keep herself from staring in disbelief at the boy standing in front of her. He looked like the same boy yet he sounded so different from the E.C.

Coleman that showed up two weeks earlier. "You can help me set up if you want."

As she went to hand him a stack of tray, Anna noticed that the tape was completely gone from his hand. Thinking back to last Friday's game, no one would have known he suffered a recent injury. Almost every pass he threw was completed. Aaron and his friend were so excited they didn't stop cheering the entire game.

Anna watched E.C. walk over to fill the pitchers with water and get the glasses ready for the drinks. He appeared to be much more comfortable about volunteering there. While Anna knew she should be glad, she caught herself biting her lip and wondering what had changed.

The serving began smoothly, but it wasn't long until Anna heard the voice of Mrs. Harris pleading, "Please… please go away and leave me alone."

When Anna looked into the dining hall, she saw Mrs. Harris standing in the middle of the room, covering her head with her arms. She immediately dropped the spatula into the pan of meat loaf and hurried out of the kitchen to her side. Anna knew the quicker she could get Mrs. Harris calmed down, the better.

"It's okay, Mrs. Harris. No one here is going to hurt you," Anna spoke gently. Mrs. Harris lowered her arms, but her grey eyes remained rimmed with white, fixed in the direction of her delusion.

Anna took a longer look at her face and saw how the years of suspicion and paranoia had taken their toll.

Pale skin fell from the protruding bones into deep hollows in her cheeks.

"Come on Mrs. Harris, eating will make you feel better. You wouldn't want that delicious peach cobbler going to waste. I happen to know it's your favorite dessert," Anna said coaxing her back toward her table. She was relieved when Mrs. Harris's face softened and her fingers relaxed.

"You're so good to me." The woman's hands shook as she tried to touch Anna's apron.

"That's what friends are for," Anna responded, reaching out to steady them for a moment. "If you're all right now, I'll go back to work."

Mrs. Harris's affirming nod gave Anna enough assurance that it was safe to return to the kitchen. She figured E.C. had left like he did the last time Mrs. Harris experienced hallucinations. But then he did offer to stay longer so he could play catch with Aaron. While Anna was still unsure what prompted such a generous commitment from him, for some reason she believed it was one he would keep.

E.C. was filling more glasses when Anna picked up the spatula to resume serving until there was no one left in line. She soon sensed the penetrating weight of E.C.'s watchful eyes on her back and wished if he had something to say to her, he would hurry and say it. In the meantime, Anna closed her eyes and inhaled slowly, summoning the energy to begin cleaning up.

"How do you do it?" E.C. finally asked.

Anna's eyelids parted at the sound of his voice and turned to find him looking soberly at her. "I don't understand what you mean."

His gaze shifted to the room filled with tables and people. "Coming here and serving them week after week. Isn't it depressing?"

Anna was careful to keep the tone in her answer from sounding too defensive. "It would be more depressing if they didn't have anywhere to go to get a hot meal. And the 'them' you refer to are people not much different than you and me."

When E.C. didn't respond right away she couldn't help but add, "A lot of these people are facing hardships that are difficult to overcome, or they have disabilities that make them unable to work. Many of them are all alone and don't have any family or friends looking out for them."

"Sorry, it's just that I've seen how some people waste money when they do have it," he said with a dose of skepticism. "Whoever that woman is at the front table has had a different shade of hair and nail polish each time I've been here. I wouldn't exactly call those necessities."

Anna looked at the front table to identify the woman he was talking about. "That's Miss Troxel. She has a niece who's a single mother struggling to make a living in a beauty shop, so she does everything she can to help, including being her best customer. It may also be the only time Miss Troxel feels a human's touch."

When Anna faced E.C. again, his head was tilted with his eyes were focused on hers. It was obvious he was thinking, though about what she didn't know.

E.C. then extended his arm in front of him. "Take off your glove and let me see your hand. I want to try something." He kept it out waiting for her to respond.

Anna hesitated, wary of his intentions, but curiosity soon won her over. She removed her glove and set her right hand precariously on his. This time there wasn't a barrier between their hands, and she could feel the rough but warm characteristics of his skin against hers.

E.C. closed his fingers over Anna's hand. "So this is human touch. Are you going to tell me this is more important than having food to eat?"

Words stuck in Anna's throat as she fought to overcome the rash of goose bumps rushing up her arm. His hand was so much bigger, so much stronger than hers. "It is for those who never experience any," the words released themselves as she withdrew her hand from his.

Anna took a moment to regain her composure before she continued, "Did you know babies in orphanages used to die because of a lack of touch? It's the first sense humans develop and the last one to leave in old age. Maybe having her hair and nails done are what's keeping Miss Troxel alive."

They stared at each other in silence a moment longer then Anna turned her attention to the people who were left finishing their meal. "See the man in the corner wearing the overalls. Everyone around here calls him Jack, though I don't think that's his real name. He used to be a school teacher, and would have had enough retirement income if his wife hadn't gotten so sick that he spent it all on medicines trying to save her. She's gone now so Jack spends his time taking care of anyone else who needs it."

E.C. remained quiet as Anna's gaze moved to the other side of the room. "At that far table is the Krauss family and their five children. They were managing just fine until Mr. Krauss was severely injured in a hit and run accident last year, and he hasn't been able to return to work yet. At least they know they can all come here to be fed."

Anna looked back at E.C. "You're one of the lucky ones. Life hasn't been as perfect for these people as it has been for you."

The same distant expression and chiseled tension Anna witnessed when she first mentioned Aaron's name returned to E.C.'s face. She felt immediate regret for her remark, though she honestly hadn't meant to say anything that would upset him. She just wanted him to understand that not everyone shared his good fortune.

"Hey guys!" Aaron stormed into the kitchen unaware of the awkward situation he was bringing relief to.

This was one time Anna was especially thankful for one of her brother's bold interruptions. His excitement was too infectious not to spread.

"Hey to you, too," E.C. said, putting up his hand to catch Aaron's high five.

"You were awesome Friday night!" Aaron jumped up in praise. "Wasn't he, Anna?"

Anna felt like the lowly peasant, expected to bow down before her royal highness, King E.C.. "It was a good game," she agreed, reluctant to provide any additional food for his ego.

E.C.'s eyes connected with Anna's before looking again at Aaron. "Are you ready to play some catch?"

Aaron's answer came in his quick retreat out of the kitchen.

E.C. laughed. "I guess that means, 'Yes'."

Anna watched him leave, realizing this had been the first time she heard him laugh. Its authenticity took her by surprise, and continued to echo in her mind. After a few minutes she walked to the window that opened to the small grass yard behind the building and watched.

E.C. was standing behind Aaron, helping him place his hand correctly on the football. Anna made sure she kept a safe distance away so as not to be seen, though close enough to understand what was being said through one of the broken panes of glass.

"The receiver cuts to the left and into the open. The quarterback steps back to throw the ball…it's in the air…and, bulls-eye, it lands right into the arms of his target. Great job Aaron."

"Can we switch places this time?" Aaron asked.

"Sure," E.C. answered, positioning himself beside Aaron to run.

Anna was intrigued by the natural interaction between the two of them and would have stayed by the window indefinitely had it not been for the haunting melody she began hearing from the kitchen. Listening more intently, Anna knew it was Louisa's voice, but the disturbing tune was one she hadn't heard before.

Walking back into the kitchen, she saw Louisa standing by the sink. "I've never heard you sing that song before."

Louisa turned to Anna with a somber expression. "It's the song that reminds me of how brave my Felix was."

"Felix... your son?" Anna was anxious to solve at least one truth about Louisa's life.

Louisa's motions appeared frozen and she didn't answer.

Anna was desperate to evoke a response from her. "Can you tell me what the words mean in English?"

Louisa slowly opened her mouth and began. "All the lads to war they've taken, woods and mountains are forsaken, lusty lads too young for dying, soldiers for their homeland sighing..."

Anna decided she didn't want to hear anymore, but Louisa kept going.

"...Far away to war they're going, blood upon the road is flowing, death awaits them undefended, so both youth and joy are ended."

Though the words stopped, their mournfulness lingered. Anna wished she had never asked what they meant. They were about war that much she understood. Louisa had talked earlier about an uprising in Hungary. "Was Felix a soldier?"

"He was never meant to be one, but when the revolution came in 1956, he was determined to go. My brave Felix fought, and then he died for us." Louisa's clenched her crippled hands into tight fists and thrust them down on the counter. "We only wanted our country back, our freedom."

Anna sensed Louisa's deep despair, but before she knew what to say, Louisa straightened up and sent her a defiant look of victory. "We escaped though, my Milo and me."

What answers Anna now had only generated more questions. Who was Hungary fighting against, and who was Milo? She assumed he was her husband, but any chance she had to find out was spoiled as E.C. and Aaron came back inside.

"Hi, Louisa," Aaron greeted her, wiping his sweaty forehead with the sleeve of his shirt.

"If it doesn't look like you've been wrung out in the wash," she chuckled with a cheerfulness that was in complete contradiction to her previous despondency.

"He kept us both running hard," E.C. added, whose shirt was just as covered with dark patches of sweat.

Anna instinctively focused on Aaron's breathing and was thankful not to see or hear anything of concern. Aaron had a tendency not to pay close enough attention to the warning signs of an asthma attack until the symptoms became much worse. Anna and the rest of the family had learned to become sensitive to them. Some might even say oversensitive.

"Well, I guess I'll be on my way. I can give you a ride home if you need one." E.C. looked at Aaron first, then Anna.

Aaron pleaded with his sister. "Please, Anna. He showed me his car. It's cool!"

Anna would do almost anything for her brother except this. "I planned to stay a little longer today to help," she lied, crossing her fingers that Louisa wouldn't call her bluff.

"Maybe some other time then," E.C. said. "See you next week, Aaron."

Everyone was quiet while he left the building, and the sound of his car's engine could no longer be heard. "Let's go, Aaron," Anna said, grabbing her violin and stack of books.

"I thought you said…," Aaron started.

"I'll explain to you later," she snapped back. "Bye, Louisa."

"Anna." Louisa's voice was cautionary. "You must let yourself trust again, especially your own feelings."

Louisa's words brought Anna to a standstill. She knew she didn't trust easily, but how could Louisa expect her to trust some privilege football player who for some unknown reason deemed playing with her brother worth his time.

When she turned and saw the imploring look of concern on Louisa's face, Anna's resolve softened. "Someday, Louisa, maybe someday…"

Chapter Seven

The next football game was out of town so Jessie came to Anna's to watch television instead. After the past couple of weeks of attending games and listening to Aaron's play by play account of his afternoons with E.C., Anna was glad not to be doing anything that had to do with football.

Anna laughed as she watched Jessie toss a piece of popcorn in the air, then lean back, and catch it with her mouth wide open.

"Bet you can't do that," Jessie challenged her.

"Are you prepared to perform the Heimlich maneuver on me if I choke?" Anna was still laughing.

"When have I not come to your rescue?" Jessie demanded acting insulted.

Jessie's question would have been funnier if it didn't hold so much truth in it. Louisa's words about the need to trust others came back to haunt Anna. She trusted Jessie, her best friend who had always been there for her. She trusted Louisa and Mr. Harmon, and of course, she trusted her family. Anna sought to think of anyone else she had admitted into the small, protected world she had created for herself, but no one came to mind.

"I'm waiting." Jessie impatiently tapped her fingers on Anna's bed where they were both sitting.

Anna sighed. "Okay, here goes." She threw the popcorn up but as she attempted to catch it, Jessie snatched it out of the air with her hand.

"Life is just full of unexpected surprises," Jessie laughed, falling back against the pillow.

"I've already had enough of those lately," Anna remarked, mostly to herself.

Jessie frowned. "I'm glad we didn't have to choose between going to the football game and watching the Miss America pageant."

Anna nodded. They tried to watch the pageant together every year. They would spend the whole evening predicting which state contestant would win. It was a tradition.

"Hey, the swimsuit competition is about to start." Jessie sat up on the edge of the bed.

Anna followed Jessie's lead and returned her attention to the small television in her room.

"You could do this, Anna," Jessie said as the first contestant came onto the stage.

Anna watched her walk across, pause, then pivot and walk back. She was a perfect vision of poise and glamour. "You're joking, right? My thighs on national television would scare away the judges for sure, not to mention all the rest of America who was watching."

Jessie shook her head. "When are you ever going to stop being so hard on yourself?"

She didn't wait for Anna's response. "Get me a comb, and then come sit down in front of me. I'm going to prove to you that you can look as good as any one of those contestants."

Anna was leery, but she knew how good Jessie was with styling hair. There wouldn't be any harm in sitting on the floor and letting Jessie's fingers work their magic.

Although Anna bristled at the thought of herself on stage in a swimsuit, when it came time for the talent portion of the pageant she had a completely different feeling. She secretly pictured herself wearing a floor length dress of plush black velvet and sparkling rhinestones, while playing her violin in front of hundreds, maybe thousands of people. Thunderous applause followed as she finished and took a bow.

A glimpse of her violin case propped up against the wall quickly dispelled Anna's fantasy. "So, who do you think is going to win?" she asked Jessie.

Jessie didn't give an answer. Instead, she jumped up, inspected Anna from the front and said, "Come on, we've got to go."

Anna didn't move. "What are you talking about? Go where?"

Jessie grabbed Anna's hand and pulled her off the floor, then out of the bedroom. "It's time."

"It's time for what? The pageant's not over yet. They're getting ready to ask the finalists their big question," Anna said already halfway down the stairs due to Jessie's pushing her from behind. "And the song, Jessie, we'll miss the Miss America song."

"See you later, Mr. and Mrs. Holmes. I'll have Anna home in an hour," Jessie hollered to her parents as they passed through the kitchen.

Anna wasn't allowed to slow down until they were inside the car and Jessie was driving. "Do you mind telling me what suddenly lit a fire under you and where it is we are going?"

Jessie threw back her head giggling. "You don't need to sound so exasperated. I can't help that I have this uncontrollable craving for a basket of fresh hot fries smothered in ketchup from Jake's Place."

"French fries? That's what this urgency is about?" Anna didn't have any trouble believing her. Jessie and food went hand in hand with each other, though you would never know it by how slender she was.

The parking lot was full but Jessie found a space across the street. "Come on, let's get inside and order before it gets any busier."

Anna looked up at the restaurant's sign, flashing alternate colors of blue and yellow. Jake's had been the local hang-out for high school students for years and was probably more crowded tonight because there hadn't been a home football game to go to. As she followed Jessie through the door, her senses were immediately flooded with the smell of hamburgers and hot grease.

"We're not going to know who won the pageant," she said, jabbing Jessie with her elbow.

Jessie leaned over and started humming the pageant's theme song softly in Anna's ear, repeating it with the words, "Here she is...."

"Jessie…," Anna froze in mid-step, "my hair. I never got to see what you did to my hair."

Her hand started to reach up to touch her head, but she quickly lowered it, hoping not to draw any attention to herself. It was too late though. As soon as Anna set her eyes on the booth in front of her, she saw them, and they saw her. E.C., Taylor, and Tonya were seated on one side with two cheerleaders and another football player she didn't know on the opposite side.

Anna couldn't read the blank expression that took over E.C's face. Either he didn't recognize her with her hair this way or he was just too stunned to see her in public looking like this.

"You've got nothing to worry about, I promise," Jessie assured her. "Come on, there's an empty booth over there by the window."

The choice was to follow Jessie or be left standing alone. Unfortunately, that meant she had to walk right by the booth containing E.C. and his friends. Anna held her breath as she hurried past, barely acknowledging E.C. with a slight nod. She pretended not to hear the comments of, "Hey, baby," and, "Who's she trying to look like?"

"Why are these people already home from the football game?" Anna asked Jessie in a low whisper as she slid onto the smooth vinyl seat across from her.

"Maybe the officials applied the mercy rule. Sometimes they'll end a game early if one team is getting beat too badly," she answered.

Anna was still thinking about the rule when a voice interrupted them, "What can I get for you girls tonight?"

Anna and Jessie looked up and were surprised to see the owner's wife standing beside their table holding a pen and order pad. "We're short on waitresses tonight," she explained, then shaking her head, "It's getting harder to keep good help these days."

"I'll have fries and a large root beer," Jessie said.

The woman held her pen poised, ready to take Anna's order. "And you?"

Anna couldn't help but notice the tired droop underlining the woman's eyes, wondering if she ever looked like that to her customers at the café. She also realized Jessie had pulled her away from home so quickly that she hadn't grabbed her purse. "I'll just have a glass of water, thank you."

Jessie shot her a frown. "Are you sure you don't want anything? I'll buy it since I did sort of force you to come here."

"No really, I'm not hungry." Maybe it was because E.C., Taylor and Tonya were in a booth not far from them, but food was the last thing Anna wanted.

The woman finished writing and started to leave when she paused to take a longer look at Anna. "My, aren't you the picture of sophistication tonight. I think you could be Madison's very own Miss America."

Anna and Jessie laughed as she walked away. It was as if she knew they had been watching the pageant.

"See, what did I tell you?" Jessie jutted her chin forward. "Your hair is definitely one of my best creations yet, if I say so myself."

Anna couldn't endure the suspense any longer. "I'll be right back. I have to see this work of art."

She chose the least conspicuous route to the bathroom and after twisting through the back tables was thankful to find it unoccupied. Standing in front of the sink, Anna held her eyes half-shut in anticipation of what the mirror would reveal. Before she had the chance to find out, the door banged against the wall as it was pushed open. Anna turned to look at who had made such an abrupt entrance and found herself looking into the face of Tonya Sterling.

Tonya walked to the only other sink. "I almost didn't recognize you with your hair that way."

Anna didn't know whether Tonya's intention was to compliment her or insult her. She began washing her hands, pretending to be busy. It wasn't until she grabbed a paper towel to dry them that she was able to glance at her full reflection. A corner of her mouth slipped up into a smile. Jessie definitely had a special gift if she could make her look this good.

"Taylor Gibbs wants to know who you are. You know he would be a good catch," Tonya said then added, "for someone like you."

This time Tonya's patronizing attitude pricked Anna's pride, and she could no longer stay silent. "Sorry, I'm not interested. I've already caught the perfect person for me."

Tonya gave her a smirk of pity then leaned in closer to the mirror to apply more mascara. "Well, it's your loss."

"Just another misfortune I have to live with," Anna responded with feigned disappointment then turned to leave knowing Jessie would be wondering what was taking her so long.

"Oh, by the way, did you see that Mrs. Carlson posted the chair assignments for our fall concert?" Tonya asked.

Anna stopped and placed a finger on her chin. "No, but let me guess. You got first chair…again, so that means you'll be our concertmaster…again."

Tonya pulled back her shoulders while lifting her chin. "You guessed right."

Anna pressed her lips together to hold in her amusement and exited the bathroom. With Louisa's help, she was slowly discovering the humor in Tonya's charades, though it was still a challenge.

Jessie gazed suspiciously at Anna when she sat back down. "I've never known you to spend that much time in front of a mirror. What took you so long?"

Anna cleared her throat and tilted her head toward Tonya who was returning to the front booth.

"Aren't you lucky," Jessie commented rolling her eyes. "Did she say anything to you?"

"She wanted to set me up with Taylor Gibbs, saying he would be a good catch for someone like me," Anna answered nonchalantly before taking a drink of the water that had arrived while she was in the bathroom.

Jessie's eyes widened. "That little vixen has got to be kidding."

Anna tried to maintain her composure and keep her mouth on her straw, but Jessie's reaction and the ridiculous picture of her and Taylor that came to mind were too comical. She grabbed a napkin to prevent water from spewing out of her mouth when she started giggling first, then coughing. "It wasn't quite as funny at the time she suggested it."

"I don't see how she can walk without tripping. She can't possibly see where she's going with her nose always stuck up in the air," Jessie speculated.

"...or read her music," added Anna. "Nothing, however, seems to get in the way of her being chosen concertmaster."

"Just maybe if her father wasn't the mayor of this town..." Jessie mused while dousing her French fries with ketchup. "Here, help yourself."

Anna's stomach lurched at the sight of greasy fried potatoes drowning in a sea of Jessie's favorite condiment. "I'll pass. One of these days they're going to start charging you extra for all the ketchup you use."

"No way." Jessie took a bite then wiped her hands with her napkin. "Oh, look, they're leaving."

Anna fought the temptation to acknowledge Jessie's observation. Instead, she watched the movement in Jessie's eyes and the grin that grew wider on her face.

"Someone couldn't keep his eyes from wandering this way," Jessie said slyly.

"Jessie, I'm beginning to detest the very thought of him." Anna heaved a sigh, glad she was facing the opposite direction.

Jessie acted surprised. "I didn't know you felt so strongly about E.C. Coleman."

"E.C...you weren't talking about Taylor?" Anna was caught in confusion.

"And that would make a difference?" Jessie eyed her curiously.

Anna thought how to best answer her question. "Only because E.C. has been volunteering at the Samaritan Center for the extra credit assignment in government, and for some reason he has taken a special interest in Aaron."

Jessie's mouth fell open. "You're just now telling me this?"

"Don't be mad at me, I was going to tell you. It just didn't seem like a big deal, and I didn't think he would stick with the assignment." Anna kept her eyes on Jessie. "It's nothing, I promise."

"Whatever you say." Jessie skewed her mouth in thought for a moment then threw both hands over her heart. "Ah, the football king meets the violin queen."

"The pauper queen is more like it." Anna's response was firm.

Her encounter with Tonya had been a painful reminder of that. How could she ever forget the time she wore a shirt from the second hand store only to find out it had once belonged to Tonya. No one would ever have known if Tonya hadn't made a point of saying she had a shirt just like it that she had given away to charity. Then in front of everyone, she tried to pry out of Anna where she got it.

Anna looked at her watch. "We'd better go if you're going to have me home in an hour like you told my parents."

"All right," Jessie complied, grabbing a few fries to go. "Come on, Miss America."

Anna felt a little more like Cinderella in a hurry to get home from the ball before the magic of her hair wore off. She had to admit it was nice having Jessie as her fairy Godmother tonight. Unfortunately, tomorrow morning she would wake up again as simply, Anna.

Chapter Eight

Anna left her hair up until the next morning when she had no choice but to finish taking down what had already fallen during her sleep. Each bobby pin she removed seemed to unlock a memory from the night before. Jessie's remark that E.C. kept looking their direction lingered the longest, staying with her thoughts while she worked all afternoon in the cafe.

She didn't mind working on Saturdays as much because she at least had the evenings to look forward to. That was when her parents had hired Jessie to come in and help during what was usually the café's busiest time. So far, the night had been much slower with not near the number of customers.

It was almost 7:30, and Jessie was clearing her latest table. Anna sat down on one of the barstools to rest and wait. She emptied the money from her apron's pocket, listening to the coins hit the counter with a hopeful ring, and then began counting.

"...twenty-five, fifty, sixty," Anna finished, adding the change to the small stack of bills. She was thankful her parents let her keep all the tip money she earned, though it never seemed enough for the hours she had to spend on her feet.

"How much have you made today?" Jessie peered over Anna's shoulder balancing an armful of dirty dishes.

Anna reached for the tin canister beside the cash register and opened it, dropping the money inside. "All of fifteen dollars and sixty cents. At this rate, I don't know how I'll ever save enough money to buy a new violin, especially since I just had to buy a new set of strings."

Jessie set the dishes on the cart and wiped her hands on her apron. "You know what they say, don't you?"

Anna lifted an eyebrow in anticipation. Jessie had yet to tell her who *they* were and what it was they said.

Instead, the front door opened, intercepting Jessie's attention and shifting the expression on her face to one of serious speculation. "I know you don't believe in fate, but I think it just walked into your cafe."

Anna tipped her head back to take a drink of water and stole a glance at whom Jessie personified as fate. She immediately froze as E. C. Coleman accompanied a woman toward a table. The woman wearing the navy blue blazer and tweed slacks had to be his mother. Her hair was neatly twisted back into a French roll, but she had the same high cheekbones and squared chin as E.C.

Questions flew through Anna's mind. What were they doing in her café and of all the empty tables, why did they have to sit down at number four? Tonight had been her turn to take the even-numbered tables.

"Jessie, I can't work that table…I just can't," she whispered frantically, holding her hand beside her face to conceal her identity.

Jessie checked the time on her watch and sucked in a breath of panic. "Anna, if I don't leave now I'm going to be late for Professor Reynolds recital. Remember, I needed to leave early tonight." She hesitated then slowly exhaled. "You know I'll stay if you really need me to."

Anna had completely forgotten about the concert at the university. Jessie had been taking lessons from Professor Reynolds and had been talking about his cello recital for the past several days. As much as Anna didn't want Jessie to leave, she couldn't ask her to stay.

"Go," Anna waved her away but Jessie balked, taking only one step back. "Jessie, I mean it. I expect you to tell me all about the concert tomorrow. Now, get out of here."

Anna would have to slay this dragon on her own, and quickly, before E.C. and his mother finished looking over their menus. This wasn't the prompt and attentive service she was used to giving her customers. Gathering her resolve, Anna tucked a loose strand of hair behind her ear, smoothed down her apron, and approached their table.

E.C.'s surprise at seeing her was apparent when he looked up from his menu. "Hello, E.C.," Anna greeted him, summoning the corners of her mouth into a polite smile.

His eyes were still busy calculating her unexpected appearance, amusing Anna with his temporary loss of words. "I didn't know you worked here," he finally said. Then as if suddenly remembering his manners, "Mother, this is Anna..."

"Holmes," Anna interjected, sensing his uncertainty about her last name.

"Anna and I met at the Samaritan Center," E.C. explained.

"It's a pleasure to meet you, Mrs. Coleman," Anna said.

A puzzled expression swept across his mother's face before she responded in a soft voice, "Same to you, Anna."

Anna had the uncomfortable feeling that she said something wrong, though she had no idea what it could have been. "Are you ready to order?"

Anna's eyes shifted back and forth between them waiting for one of them to speak up.

"Go ahead, Mom," E.C. gestured.

She looked questioningly at Anna. "I've heard this café has some of the best pies in town. Which one would you recommend?"

Anna did a visual check of the pies remaining in the lighted refrigerator case, as she savored the indirect compliment she just received. She had taken over as much of the pie making as she had time for after school and on the weekends. They tasted pretty good to her, but it was flattering to know they were gaining a reputation from others that thought so, too.

"If I had to choose a favorite I think it would be the butterscotch," she answered.

"Then, I'll have a slice of butterscotch pie with a cup of coffee, please."

Anna was relieved to see E. C.'s mother smile following her order. She then looked to E.C., who stared blankly at her in return, creating the longest period of time they had maintained eye contact.

"Evan, are you going to order?" his mother asked.

Anna almost blushed with E.C. in his obvious embarrassment at having his given name revealed. She couldn't believe she was witnessing Madison's football idol off his throne, stripped of all of his glorious pretensions by none other than his mother.

"I'll have the home-style cheeseburger with fries, please." He looked to his mother before looking at Anna again.

"Great, I'll get your order into the kitchen. It should be up shortly." Anna tore off the ticket and started to leave.

"Anna…"

She stopped and turned her head around, suddenly aware of her pounding heartbeat. For some reason the sound of her name resonated more deeply when E.C. pronounced it.

"Could you please add an iced tea to the ticket?"

"Sure," she answered, increasingly flustered by this surreal situation. There was something much different about this E.C. Coleman, unlike the one she had encountered in class and at the Samaritan Center. Her mind swam back to the name his mother had called him, "Evan."

In the kitchen, Anna kept her voice as low as possible and still be heard over the popping sizzle from the grill. "Mom, what was the first name again of this Coleman person you mentioned?"

"I only knew him as, Charlie," she said, flipping the hamburger over. "Why do you ask?"

Anna was too preoccupied to answer. If E.C. was named after his father then it was possible his initials stood for Evan Charles. It did have a nice sound to it. She went back out and busied herself with cutting the pie and pouring the drinks. By then the tray with the rest of the order was ready. Anna could see that E.C. and his mother were having a quiet conversation and wondered what they were talking about. She felt like she was intruding on their privacy, but she didn't want their food to get cold either.

"I hope you enjoy everything," she said, setting their dishes in front of them. "If I can get you anything else just let me know."

"I'm sure this will be fine. Thank you, Anna," E.C.'s mother said.

Anna went behind the counter to finish cleaning up for the evening, but managed to catch a few glances of them at their table. She was thankful Aaron was spending the night at a friend's house. If he had spotted E.C. in the cafe, the truth about the café and the fact that they lived on the floor above it would have been revealed in no time. His innocent honesty was going to be difficult to keep quiet.

She noticed E. C. and his mother stand up from the table, but instead of walking to the cash register they came toward her. She laid down her rag and met them at the counter.

"Are you ready for me to take care of your ticket?"

"We already have. I just wanted to thank you for your recommendation. That was the most delicious butterscotch pie I've ever had," E.C.'s mother answered.

"I'm glad you liked it. Maybe you can try one of the other pies another time, Mrs...."

"Mona," his mother gently interrupted then smiled. "Please, I'd like it if you called me by my first name."

"Al...alright," Anna stumbled through her response.

"We'll be back again soon, won't we Evan?" she turned to her son.

E.C. had held himself back during the exchange, but looked at Anna and nodded his answer.

"Good night, Anna," she said, leaving through the door E.C. held open for her.

Anna rubbed the chill off her arms from the rush of cool air that entered as they left. She was glad it was time to close the café down for the night. As she flipped the sign around and locked the door, her thoughts turned to what she had learned about E.C.'s mother. Other than she preferred to be called Mona and liked pie, there wasn't much else.

She walked over to the table where they had been sitting and picked up the receipt and money underneath it. They had left an extra five dollars. Anna added it to the rest of her tips from the night raising her total to twenty dollars and sixty cents. It was a bigger tip than she was used to, producing a twinge of guilt for taking it.

Anna's mother came from the kitchen as she was clearing the table. "It didn't seem quite as busy tonight."

"It wasn't. I almost didn't need Jessie's help," Anna responded then stopped to look at her. "Do you mind telling me more about this Charlie Coleman you know? I'm curious who he is."

Her mother formed a wistful smile. "You mean was. He died some time ago. I didn't know him that well, but anyone who visited his store, came away feeling as though they had met a new best friend."

Anna frowned. "What store was that?" she asked, her mind taking a quick inventory of all the stores she knew of in town.

"He owned a quaint little bookstore on Second Street, only a few blocks down from here. Stepping through that door was like stepping inside another world. The place was filled from top to bottom with books just begging to be read. I'll never forget its warmth and its intoxicating smell of ink and paper."

The quiet that followed led Anna to believe her mother had been transported back into that world. She started to say something when her mother smiled at her and continued. "What I did know about him, though, was his generosity and the boxes of books he donated to the school library every Christmas. He always delivered them himself and often stayed long enough to read a story or two to one of the classes."

Anna had forgotten about the years her mother volunteered at the school. That was during a time before her father was laid off, a time that seemed likes ages ago to her now. Charlie Coleman did sound like a nice man but not at all like someone related to E.C.. "So, what happened to the bookstore?"

Anna's mother took a deep breath. "He died so suddenly there was no choice but to close it. I felt so sorry for his wife and son that were left behind. They were just beginning to heal from the death of a newborn son when the heart attack happened. No father could have been prouder of his children, especially when he talked about how well the older one was learning to play the piano. I thought he was about your age, but I can't remember his name."

The last bit of information was proof enough to Anna that E.C. couldn't possibly be Charlie's son. E.C. was a football jock, definitely not a piano player. She yawned as the stress of the evening began to take its toll. "That's such a sad story. Whatever happened to the family?"

Her mother gave her a look of uncertainty. "Well…"

Anna covered her mouth until a second yawn was over. "Well…what?"

"I heard that Mrs. Coleman remarried," she answered.

Anna shrugged her shoulders. "I'm glad she found someone else and had a chance to be happy again."

The next words her mother spoke were more hesitant, "You're right. She was lucky to meet someone who had also lost a spouse, Clarence Baxter, the president of Baxter Industries."

Hearing the name Baxter Industries still stung and caused anxious thoughts to fill Anna's mind. It was the company that let her father go, the one responsible for her family's struggle.

Anna held her breath, almost afraid to ask. "You don't by any chance know Mrs. Coleman's, I mean Mrs. Baxter's first name, do you?"

Her mother shook her head. "No, I never met her or knew what it was."

At this point, Anna was too tired to continue sorting through the confusion. If E.C.'s mother was the Mrs. Baxter her mother was talking about then Clarence Baxter would be E.C.'s stepfather. This was more information than she wanted to deal with.

"Do you mind if I go ahead and turn in for the night?" Anna asked.

"Of course not, I'll finish up." Then as if reading Anna's thoughts she continued, "Anna, Clarence Baxter could not have prevented the layoffs. The industry was in such a state, there was no other way to save the company; otherwise the whole town would have suffered. We were only one of many families that had to start over."

Anna knew no one person was to blame for the layoffs, nor Baxter Industries. The insecurities that resulted from it, however, were taking longer to mend. She forced her tired feet up the stairs to her room and fell back onto her bed.

E.C. Coleman was becoming a greater riddle the more she was around him. Anna's head began to throb as she replayed the moment she took E.C.'s order and their eyes linked together for what seemed a timeless moment. Louisa once told her you could learn everything you needed to know about a person by looking into their eyes. Through the frame of E.C.'s long dark eyelashes Anna thought she had detected something. The question was what?

Chapter Nine

Anna bent down to wipe up a trail of spilled juice and heard the slow stride of E.C.'s steps entering the Samaritan Center kitchen. He stopped where she could see his brown leather boots through a space between the racks. She recognized them as the same ones he wore when he came into the café with his mother. After a moment, she saw him continue over to the corner and begin to fill the glasses with ice.

"Good afternoon," Anna said as she stood up beside the refrigerator.

E.C.'s back was toward her, causing him to jerk his head around. "I didn't see you when I came in."

"I was just cleaning some juice off the floor." Anna walked over to the sink to wash her hands.

E.C. stayed quiet until she was finished. "How long have you worked at the café?"

Anna was careful how she responded. "It's been a couple of years now."

"I may have to start going there more often," he said making himself comfortable against the counter.

"Everything is starting to taste the same at Jake's Place."

Anna's muscles tensed at the mentioning of Jake's Place, the location of her short-lived reign as Miss America. But the thought of waiting on E.C. again and possibly his friends unsettled her even more.

"Do you work every Saturday?" he asked.

Anna wished she knew why he wanted to know. "Not all of them," she answered, though that was barely telling the truth. She could count on one hand how many Saturdays she had missed since they opened.

There was a short lull while Anna wondered how she could find out more about his family without it looking like she was prying. It seemed unlikely that the Coleman family her mother knew about was the same one as E.C.'s, but she wanted to know for sure. They might still be related.

Anna knew it was almost time to start serving, and that she would have to act quickly. "It was nice to get to meet your mother," she said, nervous that she may be entering forbidden territory. "Do you have other family living in Cedar Grove?"

E.C. poured water into the next glass. "We're a pretty small family. Other than my mother…."

Anna was leaning on the edge of anticipation when Mr. Harmon poked his head through the kitchen window. "You all ready for a busy evening? The line's already to the corner and Mrs. Harris is seeing things again."

His interruption couldn't have come at a worse time. Anna's one opportunity was stopped dead in its tracks. As she reeled in her frustration, she looked at Mr. Harmon's face and was reminded of his innocence. Anna released a quiet sigh. "Thank you for the warning, Mr. Harmon. By the way, how's Sugar doing?"

Mr. Harmon's candid smile displayed all the crooked and missing teeth in his mouth. "Keeps my lap nice and warm, best thing that's happened to me in a long time," he answered in a tone of heartfelt sincerity. "You know, you best keep an eye out, too."

"For what?" Anna's eyebrows rose with her question.

"Sometimes, you get gifts you don't recognize 'cause you don't have to open them. One might show up at your door someday, too. And I'm not just talking about cats." He tapped his hand on the counter in front of Anna for emphasis.

Anna was aware of the truthfulness in his words. Mr. Harmon had been one of those gifts himself. Ever since they first met at the Samaritan Center, he had been gently chipping away at her defenses. Sometimes Anna felt like he could see right through her.

Mr. Harmon's steady gaze told Anna he was waiting for a response. "I'll remember that, Mr. Harmon."

Anna glanced at the clock and then at E.C. who had stopped pouring drinks and was listening in on their conversation. "We better get started serving."

E.C. took his usual place by the green beans and picked up the large spoon. "I'm ready."

The line moved quickly, challenging them to keep the trays filled. Anna did notice that Miss Troxel's hair had changed to blonde this week, and that Jack looked thinner so she placed an extra-large helping of potatoes on a plate for him. She had been too busy to remember Mr. Harmon's warning about Mrs. Harris until she spotted her a few people back. The nervous jerking of her body and fear radiating from her face were telltale signs that an outburst was imminent.

"I told you to leave me alone. What do you want from me?" her voice suddenly exploded.

Anna hurried to wipe her hands, but as she turned to leave the kitchen E.C. put his arm out to stop her. "Let me go this time."

Before she could object, he had already left and was approaching Mrs. Harris.

Mrs. Harris grabbed hold of his arm as soon as he was within reach. "Can you help me?"

"I already made him leave, Mrs. Harris," E.C. answered placing his hand on top of hers. "I made him promise to never come back here."

Mrs. Harris blinked several times, never taking her eyes off of E.C. "I don't believe I know you. What is your name?"

"It's Evan," he said without hesitation. "Why don't you sit down at a table and I'll bring you a tray of food?"

The sound of hearing his name in his own voice took Anna by surprise. First, his mother said it, and now him. There must have been a time when he didn't go by his initials and for some reason he chose not to use them with Mrs. Harris. Anna prepared a tray in slow motion while the scene played out in front of her, handing it to E.C. when he came to the window. Mrs. Harris kept her eyes on his every move, but at least the terror had faded from her expression.

If Anna thought she was confused after Saturday evening, E.C. Coleman was even more confusing to her, now. Much like watching an actor on a stage, Anna had seen him play the role as the arrogant quarterback, the personal coach to her brother, the son of a woman named Mona, and today, as the Good Samaritan. Anna couldn't believe it when he returned to the kitchen acting as if nothing unusual had just happened. Yet on his first day of volunteering, Mrs. Harris's behavior had launched him out of the center at rocket speed.

He must have sensed her contemplative stare. "Why are you looking at me like that?"

"No reason." Anna was quick to turn away and start stirring a pattern into what was left of the mashed potatoes. She didn't want to chance revealing the dilemma of her thoughts.

"By the way, I told him you already had a boyfriend," E.C. said.

The comment snapped Anna's head back around. "Told who…what?"

E.C. faced her to answer, "I told Taylor Gibbs that you already had a boyfriend."

"Tidbit?" Anna spat out.

E.C. threw his head back, "You know his nickname?"

"Not because I care to," she answered, rolling her eyes, "but you have to agree the name fits."

E.C. laughed. "I said you weren't his type anyway."

Anna looked at him and crossed her arms. "What makes you think you know what my type is?"

"I just know," E.C. said, his face now beaming with playful confidence. "Though, I feel I should tell you that Taylor suffers from a severe weakness."

For a brief instance Anna felt sorry for Taylor, that something might really be physically wrong with him. That was until she saw E.C. fighting to keep another smile from breaking. She glared back at him. "I'm guessing it can't be too severe."

"Trust me, it is." E.C. recomposed himself in an attempt to sound more convincing.

There was that word. Louisa wanted her to trust herself, now E.C. asked her to trust him. Anna put it aside for later consideration. "I'm already aware what his weakness is."

"Oh, you are." E.C. seemed taken aback. "What is it?"

"The entire female population," she answered with absolute certainty.

E.C.'s head nodded in slow affirmation. "I'm impressed, but that's only partly correct. His weakness is only for the ones he thinks are pretty."

Taylor Gibbs must not have very strict criteria for what he classifies as pretty Anna thought, especially if he paid attention to her. E.C.'s standards were sure to be much higher, making her too self-conscious to look at him again.

"Hey, Anna, catch."

Anna turned just in time to grasp the football that had been tossed at her. "Aaron! You know better than to throw the football inside the building."

"Sorry, I just wanted to show you how good I'm getting," Aaron said in his defense.

"Maybe we should take this outside now," E.C. suggested, "that is if I'm not needed in the kitchen any longer."

Anna motioned with her head toward the door and gave Aaron a forgiving smile. "Go on."

E.C. started to follow then paused. "Hey, why don't you join us?"

"Please, Anna," Aaron pleaded. "That way you can see everything E.C. and I have been working on."

Neither E.C. nor Aaron had any idea of the times she had already watched them from the corner of the window. This time, however, Aaron would know she was there, and Anna could tell how much that meant to him. "All right, I'll be out in a minute."

She put the leftover food into the refrigerator, and then checked the time. Louisa should be coming in soon to start the washing. Anna grabbed her jacket and waved to Mr. Harmon who stopped sweeping long enough to wink at her before she stepped outside. The sun sat lower in the sky now with the days passing deeper into autumn. Anna took a moment to admire the leaves' new colors against their blue canvas. Nature had been busy painting the greens of summer into bold hues of gold and scarlet.

Anna turned the corner of the building and stood on the edge of the grassy area where E.C. and Aaron were already absorbed in their game of catch. They hadn't seemed to notice her presence yet.

"The quarterback steps back to pass… he's looking downfield…, when suddenly he sees another receiver open on the play," E.C. narrated as Anna watched him lift his arm into the air. But instead of aiming the football at Aaron, he turned and aimed it toward her instead. This time the ball went through her fingers and hit her chin before bouncing on the ground in front of her.

"Timeout, there's a fumble on the play," E.C. said running over to retrieve the football. "I should have warned you. Are you all right?"

"Yes," Anna said shaking her head, "just a little dazed."

"Ready to try again?" he asked.

"Me?" Anna put her hand to her chest in protest. "I think I've already experienced enough…"

"Oh, come on, one more try," E.C. insisted.

"…*humiliation*." Anna finished her sentence in silence, regretting her agreement to join them. She looked at E.C. then at Aaron as she let out a breath of defeat. How much worse could it get?

E.C. waved for her to follow him. "Stand next to me and when I tell you to, run forward, turn to catch the ball, and then tuck it in close to your body. I promise I'll throw it easier this time."

Aaron was the one who wanted lessons on playing football, not her. Anna's palms were sweaty making her doubly sure the ball would slip right out of her hands. Right now all she wanted was the next few minutes of her life to be over with.

To Anna's surprise, she soon found herself standing in the middle of the field with her hands gripped to the football.

"Run before Aaron gets you," E.C. cautioned her.

Anna turned to see Aaron coming full speed toward her, but it was too late. Aaron had already covered too much ground.

"Gotcha," he said, wrapping his arms tightly around her waist.

That was all the force it took to unbalance Anna and cause them to fall to the ground together in one heap.

Aaron rolled off Anna as E.C. came over to offer his help. "Hey, great tackle."

Anna sat up and gave Aaron her best *you're going to pay for this* look.

"I really didn't mean to knock you over," he said, skewing his face in self-defense.

"Don't forget I'm still bigger than you are," she said before giving in to a broad grin and looking at E.C. with the corner of her eye. "But he is right, that was a great tackle."

Anna brushed the grass off of her jeans and rustled Aaron's hair. "That's all the football for today. We have to get my things and go home."

"Head for the door, veer left, and I'll throw you one more pass," E.C. offered.

Aaron ran forward with more self-assurance than Anna had ever witnessed in him. She knew it wouldn't matter to him if E.C. was related to the same Baxter that caused her father to lose his job. As hard as Anna tried to forget that part of her past, every time she went home she was haunted by how much their lives had changed because of it.

"You're lucky," E.C. said, watching Aaron catch the ball.

The ironic timing of E.C.'s comment wasn't lost on Anna. "How is that?"

"Having a little brother," E.C. answered.

"It's obvious you don't have one," she teased.

E.C.'s eyes lowered. "No, I don't."

Anna felt horrible. The words slipped out before she remembered what her mother told her. If by any chance he was Charlie Coleman's son, then his little brother died. She wished she possessed telepathic powers so she could know what he was thinking.

They entered the kitchen to find Louisa soaping up the pots and pans. When she saw them the wrinkles on her forehead furrowed deeper with concern. "What is scattered in your hair, Anna? Did you fall down?"

"In a manner of speaking," Anna answered, reaching up to feel the strands of her hair for remnants from Aaron's tackle.

"Here, let me help." E.C.'s hand began to gently pull bits of dry grass out of her auburn waves.

"There, I got most of them," he said, their eyes briefly passing each other.

Anna felt the same sensation wash over her as when he held her hand. It was at the same time both breathtaking and frightening. She just hoped her face wasn't turning red.

In the meantime, Aaron went to stand beside Louisa, only he was more fascinated by the scientific properties of soap bubbles than helping her wash dishes.

"I think Louisa will get finished with her work a lot faster without your help, Aaron. Come on, we need to go home anyway," Anna said.

"Anna, tell me again when you leave for the competition?" Louisa asked.

The question troubled Anna. She had just reminded Louisa about the All-District audition during her lesson earlier. As she looked at Louisa deciding what to say, she observed a distinct quiver in her motions. Anna had always been curious how her gnarled fingers could lift the large stainless steel pans to wash them, but Louisa insisted hot water and singing gave her all the strength she needed.

"Are you going to answer?" E.C. turned to Anna.

Anna shoved aside the gnawing uneasiness she felt about Louisa's health and softly responded. "Remember, it's this Saturday, Louisa," she said, hoping to quickly jog her memory and keep E.C. from becoming any more involved in the conversation.

Louisa's eyes appeared to be playing out an inner struggle. "Yes, of course. I remember now," she finally answered in a satisfied tone.

Anna's relief turned out to be premature.

"What competition is this?" E.C. asked.

Before Anna could open her mouth, Louisa took charge of the question, defying any previous confusion she might have had. "It's for the All-District honor orchestra, and I know deep down in my bones that she is going to make it. Few people play their music with the passion Anna possesses."

Anna was stunned. This was the first compliment she had ever heard from Louisa.

Can we go home now?" Aaron's impatience jarred Anna back to the present.

"You bet." She dared to look at E.C. to say goodbye, hoping she wouldn't have to make up another excuse should he offer them a ride home again.

E.C. was already looking at her in a thoughtful manner. "I guess I'll see you all later." He took a few steps then turned back and smiled. "By the way, that was a nice catch."

Anna gave him a half-smile in return. "Thanks," she said and watched him continue out the door.

She started to gather her belongings when a pan fell to the floor producing a loud clang. "Louisa! Are you okay?"

"It is nothing, I am all right," she motioned, trying to dispel any worry. She bent over to pick up the pan and placed it on the shelf.

Anna knew something was not all right. Something hadn't been all right for weeks. "Maybe you should go to the doctor for a checkup."

"No, no doctors. It is just my old body." Louisa shook her head. "I'll be fine. You will come see me after the try-outs?"

"Of course." Anna knew the discussion was over. Louisa could defeat an army with her sense of pride and determination.

Aaron ran ahead of her out the door, forcing Anna to walk faster than she wanted to. This evening had been different and nice. She and E.C. had treated each other like friends. Maybe she had been too unfair in her judgment of him in the beginning and drawn her sword too quickly. She only knew how much lighter she felt when she wasn't wearing a coat of armor to protect herself.

They were almost to the café when Anna called Aaron back to walk beside her. "So, what do you really think about E.C.?"

Aaron's response couldn't have been faster. "If I had a big brother, I would want him to be just like him."

Anna expected him to say nothing less.

They entered the café, ringing the bell as the door opened. Had either of them turned around while they were walking, they might have noticed the blue car following a block behind them their entire journey home.

Chapter Ten

Anna stood at her locker, thankful it was Friday and school was finished for the week. Except that it also meant that she would be leaving for All-District auditions the next morning. She glanced around her locker door to see if Jessie was coming yet and cringed at whom she saw instead. E.C., Taylor, and Tonya were in a group gathered outside a classroom a few doors down from her.

The team never practiced on game day, but Anna wished they would have chosen somewhere else to hang out. The only way to exit the hallway was to walk right past them. She couldn't continue to wait there indefinitely.

After another peek, Anna decided Jessie was running more than just a little late and may have forgotten to meet her. Being as inconspicuous as she could, Anna lifted the handle and closed the door, completely exposing her identity. She only hoped they would be so absorbed in themselves, they wouldn't notice her.

With a mind of absolute dread, Anna turned and willed her feet forward, keeping her eyes set straight ahead. E.C.'s back was facing her so at least he wouldn't know she was coming. Seeing him at school among his friends was very different from seeing him at the Samaritan Center. They had yet to speak to each other in class or in the hallway, only nodding whenever their eyes met. She didn't want to appear unfriendly since they at least had Aaron's best interest in common, but she couldn't bring herself to look his direction with the others there. It was obvious when their conversation lulled that they were watching her go by.

"Won't I be lucky if she makes All-District, too," Tonya said with heavy sarcasm and plenty of volume to ensure that Anna heard her.

Anna wanted to tell her the feeling was mutual but held on to her composure instead. She turned the corner and was halfway to the front door when she heard steps running behind her.

"Anna... wait up."

Anna looked back and saw E.C. coming toward her with a piece of paper in his hand. "I'm not sure your friends would approve," she said once he reached her.

E.C. shrugged his shoulders. "If you're talking about Tonya, just ignore her."

Anna had spent years trying to ignore Tonya. With Louisa's help it had become easier to rise above Tonya's petty jabs, but Anna still looked forward to graduation when they would never have to cross paths again.

"Here, you dropped this. I thought you might need it." E.C. held up the piece of paper in front of her.

Anna glanced at the stack of papers in her arms and realized a sheet of her music must have slipped off. It was the first page to her favorite of the three pieces she would be auditioning with for All-District. She took the paper and stuck it more securely between two of her books.

"Thanks, though I doubt having it will make a difference. I probably won't make it anyway," she replied, unintentionally revealing her curse of self-doubt.

E.C. gave her a look of reproach. "Is this for the audition you were talking about with Louisa?"

Anna nodded.

"I heard what she said about your playing. Don't you remember?" he asked.

Of course she did. She had repeated Louisa's exact words, over in her mind what seemed like a million times. When Anna tried to answer, her eyes became fastened with his and she couldn't move them or her mouth.

"I do," he said with a tone that stirred Anna's tangled emotions.

Why would he care about her audition or anything Louisa had said to her? She was sure to be nothing more to him than someone he met volunteering, while Louisa was just an old woman with an accent that sang foreign songs while she washed dishes.

"There's where you ran off to," Taylor's voice intruded from the end of the hall, breaking the spell that had captured her.

"I've got to go now," Anna said, suddenly finding her voice.

"Are you bringing Aaron to the game tonight?" E.C. asked as Anna backed away.

"I'll try," she answered, leaving quickly as Taylor's figure fast approached them. Even though E.C. had told Taylor she wasn't his type, Anna didn't want to risk being an object of his weakness again.

She knew she shouldn't go to the game, having to work in the café first and then needing to practice before her auditions the next morning. Madison was almost guaranteed to win again, the way their season had been going.

The air, though cool when it first hit her face, felt good when she stepped out of the school. "Anna," she heard a voice holler at her. When she turned, she saw Jessie running toward her from the parking lot.

Anna started to act miffed until she detected the glow radiating from Jessie's face. "Where have you been?"

Jessie took a few steps alongside Anna to catch her breath before answering. "You know Kyle don't you, the string bass player in orchestra? He asked me to walk to his car with him, and I kind of forgot I was supposed to meet you. Forgive me?"

Anna slid her chin sideways and eyed Jessie's smile, "You were late because of a boy, leaving me your best friend, stranded?"

"Someday, you'll understand," Jessie said then poked Anna with her elbow. "Maybe you already do."

Anna shook her head. "I'm sure I've scared away any potential boy if there ever was one, and Taylor Gibbs doesn't count." She became quiet then added. "I wish you were trying out for All-District."

"I wish I was, too" Jessie echoed. "I would be if my aunt wasn't getting married the same weekend as the performance. The wedding is going to be so romantic, though, I can't wait."

Jessie's new attitude bewildered Anna. She had never talked about boys and weddings before with such interest. But then Jessie never had a problem sharing her feelings even if it meant making herself more vulnerable.

"Are we still on for the game tonight?" Jessie asked.

"I think I should stay home this time. I have to be at the school so early in the morning to meet the bus, and I want to practice over my pieces again." More and more, Anna was regretting her agreement to audition.

"You're the most prepared person going tomorrow. C'mon, it will help keep your mind off the audition for awhile," Jessie insisted.

Anna's hesitation was all the answer Jessie needed. "Good, that settles it," she said before letting out a low whistle. "Now there's a possibility for you."

Anna had no idea what she was talking about until she followed the shift in Jessie's focus. Turning away from them at the corner was E.C.'s blue Camaro.

"Have you completely lost all your senses? I'm sure if it wasn't for Aaron, he wouldn't care I existed." Anna knew that may not be a fair evaluation of his feelings. The way he had been acting lately showed he did care a little, but only as a friend, definitely not a girlfriend.

"How is their little game of catch going anyway?" Jessie gave her a sly smile.

Anna couldn't hold back a grin as she remembered what had taken place a couple of days earlier. She must have looked ridiculous being tackled by someone half her size. "Aaron loves the attention. It's been great for him."

She almost included that it seemed to be good for E.C., too, but then changed her mind. Maybe she was making more out of the relationship than there really was.

"Hmmm," Jessie sounded. "And you've even met his mother."

"Jessie, you can stop your wild imaginings." Anna was adamant.

Jessie threw a hand up in the air. "Okay, you win for now. I'll be by the café to pick you and Aaron up at 7:00."

Anna released a quiet sigh. "We'll be ready."

She hadn't been able to tell Jessie she didn't need any help keeping her mind off the audition. For the past several days, it was keeping her mind on it that had been the problem.

Chapter Eleven

Auditions were being held in a school a couple of hours away from Madison. Anna expected the early morning bus ride to be miserable, and so far she was right. After a sleepless night following the game, she crawled out of bed with a throbbing headache and squeamish stomach. Her mother offered to fix breakfast, but Anna declined, afraid her body would reject any food she managed to swallow. The constant jostling of the bus was doing nothing but making her feel worse.

Anna was glad she wasn't sharing a seat with anyone. Tonya insisted on sitting by herself at the back of the bus while Kyle, Jessie's new boy interest, sat across the aisle with his portable CD player and headphones on. His eyes were closed, portraying the perfect picture of calm, while she was busy fighting off alternating waves of hot and cold.

Desperate for a distraction from her anxiety, Anna forced her thoughts back to the football game the night before. The outcome was just as she had predicted. Madison scored a string of touchdowns early in the first half that sealed their victory. Anna had to admit E.C. was a great quarterback, especially since he had thrown a pass that even she could catch.

She was glad her brother was with her at the game even if he did keep waving to E.C., convinced he could see him in the stands. At least she had someone to cheer with. Jessie hadn't told her that Kyle would be joining them. Once he did, Jessie only bothered to look at the scoreboard twice, once at the end of the first half and once at the end of the second half. For the rest of the time, her attention was devoted entirely to him.

At one point Anna glanced through the crowd and saw the boy that had spoken to her at the first game she went to. He seemed friendly enough, but she wasn't interested in complicating her life with a boyfriend. She was tired of hearing all the talk at school concerning break-ups and make-ups. Then Anna's eyes fell on Jessie and Kyle and she caught the murmuring edge of their conversation. Envy opened the door, but she refused to enter. If Jessie was happy, she would be happy for her.

"We'll be arriving in Deer Creek shortly, for those of you who have been trying to get in some extra sleep this morning."

Mrs. Carlson's announcement snapped Anna back to the present and the reason for this agonizing bus trip. Her stomach was rumbling now, and she wished she had brought something with her to eat.

"Hey, Anna, you don't look so good," Kyle remarked, having opened his eyes and stretched his arms.

"I think I'm hungry," she said, aware that the rumbling was getting louder.

"Hold on. I've got just what you need." Kyle rummaged through his backpack, and then pulled out a package. "Here it is. I have for you the perfect gift of nourishment."

Anna inspected the squished contents of his outstretched hand. "It's a honey bun, Kyle."

"Like I said, nourishment at its best," he stated with almost as much endearment as he had shown Jessie at the football game.

"That's all right, you can keep it," she declined.

"No, you have to take it or I wouldn't be fulfilling my duties." Kyle continued to persuade her with one hand pressed to his chest and the other one holding the package closer to her face.

The role he was playing suddenly became evident. "Jessie put you up to this didn't she?"

"She just asked me to look out for you. It's my last one, but I've managed to survive on only two before." Kyle bent down on one knee in the aisle. "Please, take it."

Anna couldn't resist his gallant efforts any longer and reached out to accept his sacrifice of food.

"What kind of pathetic display of chivalry is this?" Tonya asked, having unexpectedly shown up in the aisle next to Kyle.

Kyle answered matter-of-factly, "The kind shown to real princesses, not self-appointed ones."

Tonya responded with a smirk. "Well, I don't care what you think. I need to move to the front, and you're in my way."

Kyle smiled at Anna with a slight bow of his head before slowly getting back in his seat.

Anna was beginning to understand now why Jessie liked Kyle so much. She tore open the plastic package and bit into the sweet, sticky pastry. Once she started eating she couldn't stop. By the time she finished the last bite, her stomach felt much better.

"I see the color coming back into your face at this very moment," he observed with a look of satisfaction. "You know I didn't mean what I said earlier about you not looking good. Nothing could make a natural beauty such as you…"

"Kyle, it's okay," Anna cut him off, grinning at his irrepressible manner. "Thank you for sharing your food."

The bus slowed down as it made a turn into the Deer Creek high school parking lot.

"Are you ready for this?" Kyle asked when the bus came to a complete stop.

"As ready as I'll ever be," she answered, pulling her violin out from under the seat.

Kyle's eyes were gentle as he looked at her arms wrapped around her case. "You're going to do great you know. All the judges will hear is how wonderful you play the music."

Anna managed to hide her embarrassment from his well-intentioned encouragement and lifted up her chin. "I hope so."

They walked inside the building together and found the gymnasium that was designated as the warm-up area. Several people were already practicing their music, creating a layer of dissonance that was difficult to block out. Others looked like they had slept there all night, sprawled on the floor with blankets and pillows. Anna presumed they were either given later audition times or were extraordinarily confident. She checked the time on her watch.

"I've got an hour, how about you?" Anna looked at Kyle.

"About the same," he answered while taking a visual tour of the room. Kyle then pointed to an unoccupied area underneath the basketball goal. "Let's set up camp over there."

"Where will I find the section cuts for my music," she asked.

"If it's like last year, they're posted in the hallway. Why don't you go look and I'll wait here," he offered.

Anna nodded then exited the gym. She spotted a small cluster of people reading something attached to the wall and eased her way into an opening in the group. While the entire pieces had to be learned, it wasn't known until the day of the audition which sections had been selected to be played. The more Anna studied the sections, the more astonished she became. Louisa's predictions were all correct except one.

When Anna returned to the gymnasium, Kyle had a chair and music stand ready for her, and was already warming up on his bass. She realized then the friend he was quickly becoming, even though that meant she would be sharing Jessie.

"Mrs. Carlson came by and said some of the numbers ahead of me didn't show up. That means I have to play earlier than my scheduled time. I'll try and catch up with you before you have to go," he said.

"Good luck." Anna tried say with a smile as he left. She then got out her violin and attempted to tune it amidst the sounds of discord filling her ears. After running through all of her selections, she became too restless to sit any longer and was only getting more nervous listening to everyone else.

Checking her watch one more time she decided to find the room she had been assigned to audition in. Anna walked down the hallway looking for Room 105. As Anna got closer to the door, she saw Mrs. Carlson speaking to Tonya who was preparing to go in. She wondered if Mrs. Carlson would have anything to tell her before she played.

Anna saw the list showing the order of students for that room and ran her finger down the numbers. She found Tonya's first and then hers. Five more until it was her turn to go. She leaned against the cold brick for support, thankful that a code of quiet was maintained outside the audition rooms. The playing coming from behind the closed door was barely audible but she was certain Tonya was doing well and would be chosen. Anna figured there wasn't anything Tonya wanted that she didn't get.

The door opened and Tonya walked out, barely glancing at Anna as she went past. "Have fun in there.

I heard the judges are brutal this year," she said without slowing down her steps.

Anna fought hard to keep the statement from poisoning her concentration. She thought back to her last conversation with E.C. and Louisa's bold proclamation about her playing ability. Anna suddenly felt foolish for believing Louisa's words.

"Good, I'm not too late," Kyle whispered, sneaking up behind Anna.

Anna jerked around in surprise at his unexpected appearance. "You're already finished?"

Kyle nodded then smiled for reassurance. "Don't worry. It will be over before you know it."

Mrs. Carlson, who was still standing close to the door, motioned for Anna to come to her.

Anna's feet hesitated and she sucked in air like it was going to be her last breath. "Here I go."

Mrs. Carlson put a hand on Anna's arm as soon as she reached her. "You can do this, Anna. Just play exactly like you do in class. Now, go for it," she added with a squeeze.

The next few minutes became a blur in Anna's memory. It was as if she had to pull herself out of a dream to know she was finished. Her ears tried to recapture the sounds her violin had just made but they couldn't.

Kyle met her as she came out of the audition room. They were heading back to the gymnasium in silence when Anna's stomach embarrassingly announced its desire for more food.

"I'm sorry I don't have another honey bun to offer you," he said sounding truly remorseful.

Anna couldn't contain the stress of the past few days any longer and burst out laughing, feeling the knots of tension melt away in her shoulders. She had played her violin the only way she knew how. There was nothing left for her to do but wait.

Chapter Twelve

"Louisa!" Anna knocked on the front door of the Samaritan Center then pressed her ear against the wood for any sounds of movement from inside. "Louisa!" she called out again.

Since it was Sunday and the center was closed, Anna decided Louisa was probably in her bedroom on the other side of the building. She turned to start walking toward the back door when the familiar creaking of hinges prompted her to stop.

"Anna?" Louisa's voice rang with concern. "What is so urgent?"

Anna moved closer to Louisa to speak, but her words were barely audible. "I did it, Louisa. I made All-District."

The corners of Louisa's mouth softened into a smile as she slowly nodded, "I know."

Anna's mind was busy trying to figure out who could have already told her, when Louisa answered her quiet bewilderment. "I've known for some time now from in here," she said, placing her hand on her chest.

It seemed like Louisa's heart was always speaking to her, Anna thought, or maybe it was simply that Louisa listened to hers more often.

Her body was still restless with energy from the day before and the shock from Mrs. Carlson's phone call telling her she made it. "Do you feel like going for a walk? It's a beautiful day and I doubt we'll have many more like it before it gets too cold."

"Wait here while I get my sweater. I want to show you my favorite place," Louisa answered as if Anna's energy had spilled into her.

Anna had no idea where that might be until Louisa returned and suggested they walk down Roosevelt Avenue. It was then that she realized they were headed for the city park located by the old train station.

"Let's sit over there," Louisa suggested, pointing to a bench on a hill that overlooked the entire park. She looped her arm through Anna's and started up the incline, taking small measured steps.

"I like to come here as often as I can," she said after they sat down.

"By yourself?" Anna was already alarmed about the declining state of Louisa's health. She didn't like the idea of her going anywhere alone.

"You don't think I should stay inside the center all day do you?" Louisa questioned in self-defense. "It's out here in God's creation where I can feel every one of my blessings."

Anna watched Louisa's expression suddenly grow distant as if her spirit had been transported to another time and place. She didn't want to appear as if she were eavesdropping and looked away toward the pond where a sampling of geese and ducks were creating ripples of patterns across the water. Their movements appeared effortless, but only because the paddling of their feet was hidden below the edge of the water's surface. Anna realized how similar their swimming was to performing a piece on her violin. The music should sound effortless no matter how hard she had to work to play it.

"Have you ever seen a crane dance?" Louisa asked, returning to the moment as suddenly as she had left.

Anna frowned, thrown by the peculiarity of the question. She shook her head, having no idea what Louisa was talking about.

"In Hungary, Milo and I went to a place called Hortobagy every autumn to watch the cranes fly in. Sometimes there would be thousands of them, stopping to rest on their journey south for the winter. While they were stopped, they would always dance for us," Louisa started to explain.

Anna raised her eyebrows in response, having never heard of a bird that could dance. "How do you know they're dancing?"

Louisa smiled. "They lift up their wings and leap in the air, throwing their heads back and trumpeting. They even do pirouettes and then bow. I've never seen another creature celebrate their existence with such elegance and joy."

Louisa dropped her shoulders and settled back against the bench. "Milo and I wanted to be just like the cranes. Did you know that once they find their mate, it's for life?"

Anna waited while a swelling breeze wove through the branches of the willow tree beside them before she answered. "No, I didn't." Then not wanting to miss an opportunity to find out more she gathered up her courage to ask, "Would you tell me more about Milo?"

Wistfulness had gathered in Louisa's eyes when she turned to answer Anna. "Milo was the gentlest man I knew and the best teacher of history at the university. He loved sharing his knowledge, but there was never any doubt that Felix and I were the most important things in his life."

Anna hurt for Louisa. She had lost a husband and a son, all the family Anna was aware she had. "I'm sorry you're alone now."

Louisa directed her eyes again at Anna. "But I am not alone. I have you."

Anna was basking in the warmth of that acknowledgement when Louisa's hand reached out and touched her.

"Besides, I talked to Felix again today," she said, seeming to press the words into Anna's arm. "This time Milo was with him. He told me it wouldn't be much longer now until I see him again."

"But Louisa…" Anna stopped to wrestle with the importance of challenging Louisa's confusion with reality. Who was she to risk destroying any of the few comforts of life Louisa had left, real or imagined?

"I think I should walk you home now," Anna decided instead to suggest.

Louisa straightened up. "Yes, I must be getting myself ready."

Anna stood to assist her, but Louisa was already on her feet moving in haste down the hill. Whatever Louisa was getting ready for she was in a hurry to do so.

The only sounds filling the space of their return walk to the center was the occasional engine from a passing car or the scraping edges of dried leaves as they blew across the sidewalk. The way Louisa's mind had been switching in and out of reality made Anna afraid to look too closely at her. What if the last two years had been some kind of cruel trick? Louisa had been seeing ghosts of her son and husband. If Anna didn't know better, she might wonder if Louisa was a ghost, too, by the mysterious way she appeared in her life.

Once they returned to the Samaritan Center, Anna waited for Louisa to unlock the door. "I have some new music to start learning for the clinic and performance next weekend. When I see you on Wednesday, we can work on it," she said stepping back to leave.

Louisa was nodding her agreement from the doorway when her eyes suddenly widened and she laid her hands together on her chest. "I can almost see them!"

Anna's head twisted from side to side as a cloud of uneasiness descended upon her. "See who?" she dared to ask expecting the answer to be Milo and Felix.

"Not who," Louisa chuckled, dismissing Anna's question with a wave of her hand. "Why it's your wings," she said with absolute certainty then closed the door.

Anna's movements were frozen as she stared at the solid wood panel in front of her. She was scared. There was no denying Louisa's worsening condition any longer, now that she was seeing more than just visions of memories. Mr. Deacon would have to be told.

Turning away from the center, Anna felt a sudden impulse to glance over her left shoulder. Of course nothing was there, that would have been ridiculous. For the remaining distance home, however, Anna's curiosity kept tempting her to check. Each time she asked herself the same question. Just what kind of wings did Louisa think she saw?

Chapter Thirteen

Anna arrived for her lesson the next Wednesday in a state of inner turmoil. She struck the strings of her violin with a sharp downward movement, grimacing at the unpleasant sound it produced.

"I don't know which is worse, this bow or this violin," she said, shaking them both in a fit of frustration. "It must have been a mistake that I made All-District."

In the silence that followed, Anna felt Louisa's penetrating gaze. When she gathered the courage to face her, Louisa remained quiet, washing Anna with guilt. The truth was that today the problem wasn't with either her bow or her violin, it was with her. She felt like a traitor, like she had betrayed Louisa by telling Mr. Deacon about the hallucinations she seemed to be having.

Anna was only hoping he would convince her to have a check-up with a doctor. Now, she wasn't sure she had done the right thing. Louisa was perfectly lucid this afternoon. Who was she, Anna Holmes, to pass judgment on what she couldn't see?

"I'm sorry for wasting your time today," Anna apologized.

"I would know if my time was being wasted," Louisa responded firmly and then fixed her gaze back on the music.

Anna sensed the unspoken expectation for her to try the piece again and returned the violin underneath her chin. She couldn't take her words back from Mr. Deacon, but she could play better for Louisa. She owed her that and much more.

Louisa closed her eyes while listening to the music then opened them with an approving nod after the last note faded. "That is enough for today. You will be ready for this week-end. Besides the football player will be here soon."

Anna lifted her head up from putting her violin back into its case. "That only matters where Aaron is concerned. I'm glad he's too young to understand that E.C. comes from a whole different world than us."

"Ah, but maybe you are wrong, Anna. You haven't traveled far enough outside of your world to learn about his."

Louisa's words took a moment to sink in. By then, Louisa had already left the room. Anna admitted she spent most of her time between the Samaritan Center and the café, but how could she be wrong? Louisa would have to be blind not to see that E.C. came from far more privileged circumstances than she did. While they were at least getting along now, her experiences so far had taught her that these two worlds rarely mixed.

Anna started busying herself with her normal Wednesday routine while trying to keep thoughts of Louisa and the upcoming orchestra clinic out of her mind. The cooks were already preparing the meal, and Mr. Harmon was setting out extra chairs. Since it was the end of the month, more people tended to show up, having already run out of what money they had.

She had just finished filling salt and pepper shakers when she accidentally stepped back into a body behind her. Anna gasped when she turned around. "Mr. Harmon, are you okay?"

Mr. Harmon nodded his head. "Don't you worry, no harm done. It would take more than a little bump to bring this grumpy old man down."

"I bet you've never been grumpy a day in your life," Anna teased.

"Let's just say I've been less grumpy since Sugar came around," he said with a wink. "Hey, I got a new joke for you."

Anna crossed her arms and grinned in preparation for Mr. Harmon's simple style of humor. "Okay, I'm ready."

"What did the cowboy say when he found out his dog left?" Mr. Harmon asked with a drawl.

Even if Anna knew the right answer, she wouldn't deprive Mr. Harmon the visible pleasure he got out of telling her. She shrugged her shoulders. "I have no idea."

Mr. Harmon's mouth formed a crooked smile. "Doggone!" he emphasized with a snap of his fingers.

Anna tossed her head back and laughed more at Mr. Harmon than the joke itself. It felt good as she felt the load of all her worries lighten. Mr. Harmon joined in the moment with her.

"Looks like I missed out on something funny," interrupted a familiar deep voice.

"Well, doggone it," Mr. Harmon said.

E.C. looked bewildered as Anna laughed even harder at Mr. Harmon's response.

"Sugar told me that one. She's good at telling dog jokes," Mr. Harmon said before he walked away.

Anna was in a state of enchanted disbelief as she watched him leave. Maybe she was the one who was really crazy since she didn't talk to animals, hear voices or see people and objects that weren't there.

"Who is this Sugar you two keep talking about?" E.C. asked, drawing Anna's attention back to him.

"His cat," she answered, suppressing her amusement at his still puzzled expression. "But I'll have to explain later. It's time we get ready to start serving."

E.C. was quiet while Anna filled the warming compartments with food, though her eyes kept meeting his. There wasn't any denying that he was good-looking and that he had surprised her with his kindness toward her brother and Mrs. Harris, but she had no expectations for anything more in their relationship. After all, the volunteer assignment and football season were almost over. When would she even see him other than in class? They barely talked at school because he was usually surrounded by his friends, a circle she didn't belong in. Louisa just didn't understand.

"Congratulations," E.C. broke the silence as he readied himself by the green beans.

It took a moment for Anna to realize E.C. was talking about the All-District audition. He must have heard about the results from Tonya. Anna didn't want to know what else she might have told him. She was sure Tonya wasn't looking forward to spending the upcoming weekend together. The scowl on her face when Mrs. Carlson announced their names to the class was proof enough of that.

"Thanks," Anna said taking a longer look at E.C. It was then she noticed the disheveled hair and tag sticking out from the neck of his shirt. He was a complete contradiction to his usual neat appearance.

Her observation didn't go unnoticed and he ran his hand over his head. "You'll have to excuse how I look. Coach practiced us extra hard today getting ready for the game. If we win this one, we'll get to go to the state playoffs."

"Too bad, it's out-of-town. Aaron will have to be content listening to it on the radio."

"I hope someone shows up to cheer us on. This team is known to have a pretty mean crowd."

"I'm sure there will be a lot of Madison fans there," Anna reassured him as the first people in line came to the counter.

Anna kept hearing comments as the trays were handed out about how the wind was picking up and the temperature was dropping outside. She thought ahead to the winter season when it came to the end of each meal and the center had to lock the door for the evening. It was always difficult to watch those who had lingered in the warmth of the building, leave with little more than a long-sleeved shirt covering their arms. Anna could only hope they found heated shelter somewhere else out of the cold.

The afternoon seemed to drag on longer than most to Anna, most likely because she was still worn out from the auditions and from worrying about Louisa. She managed to suppress one yawn but couldn't hold the second one back, quickly placing her hand over her mouth to cover it.

"You don't have to hang around here and wait for Aaron. I don't mind taking him home after we've finished playing catch," E.C. offered.

In Anna's tired stupor she almost forgot that she couldn't let him do that. She drew in a deep breath to renew her resistance. "Thanks, but it gives me a chance to give Louisa some extra help. I'll manage to stick around," she said before another yawn overcame her. "Besides, Aaron should be here any minute."

E.C.'s face was a blend of thoughtful amusement, whipping up Anna's self-consciousness. She wasn't really hiding anything; there just wasn't any reason E. C. ever needed to know where they lived.

By then Aaron came running in the kitchen, giving E.C. his special high five.

Anna stretched her neck toward the window to catch a glimpse outside. It looked like the clouds had grown heavier. "It's a good thing you wore your jacket, I heard it's getting colder out there," she said then added, "I don't think you ought to play very long today."

Aaron sent Anna a silent but strong, "I'll be okay" glare.

It was surprising their mother even let him come. But then Anna had noticed her overprotective tendencies easing up over the past few weeks, ever since Aaron met E.C. and was going to the football games. Occasionally, her mother still asked if she knew yet whether E.C. was Charlie Coleman's son, and Anna still didn't have an answer for her. She wasn't going to do or say anything to E.C. that might jeopardize the time Aaron had left to spend with him.

"Let's go pal," E.C. nudged Aaron. "We don't want to waste any time."

No one could be happier for Aaron than Anna as she watched them leave the kitchen. She could hear Louisa humming down the hallway, and it reminded her of the conversation she had with Mr. Deacon. Louisa had made such a difference in her life. Anna only wanted to take care of her in return. Thankfully, Mr. Deacon didn't act too alarmed by what she told him and promised he would check in on her.

"It is much chillier in my room today," Louisa said upon entering the kitchen. "It may be time for Mr. Deacon to check the heater, you think?"

"Yes," Anna answered, uncomfortable with the knowledge that Louisa would be talking to Mr. Deacon soon but not just about turning on the heat.

"You are quiet today, first in your lesson and then now," Louisa observed. "Everything is all right at the cafe and with Aaron?"

"Everything is fine, I'm just extra tired that's all," Anna said, propping up her chin with her elbows on the counter then closing her eyes. Almost immediately, she was inside a dreamlike scene of sitting in an orchestra with people all around her playing the music she had been practicing so hard to learn. It was as if she was already at All-District.

"Anna!"

The panicked voice jolted Anna to her feet while her mind grappled with the urgent calling of her name.

"Anna!" E.C. came rushing into the kitchen carrying Aaron, and then set him down.

"What is it?" Her vision was blurred from fear, and she had a difficult time focusing on either of their faces waiting for the answer. Then she heard it, the wheezing and raspy coughs of Aaron struggling to get his breath.

Anna lowered herself to Aaron's eye level and sought to create the most soothing voice she could manage. "It's okay Aaron, I want you to stay calm," she commanded, speaking as much to slow down the racing beat of her own heart. "Where is your inhaler?"

"Check inside his jacket," Louisa said.

Anna looked at Louisa then back at Aaron's arms covered only by a t-shirt. "Where did you put your jacket?"

"Outside," he whispered between short labored breaths.

When Anna turned to E.C., he was already running out the door. In what seemed like no time at all, he returned with the jacket in his outstretched hand for her to grab.

Anna fumbled with the zipper pocket then pulled the inhaler out, shook it and pulled off the cap before handing it to Aaron. He then pressed the dispenser into his mouth, taking a breath at the same time.

"Is he going to be all right?" E.C. asked.

Anna kept her eyes on Aaron's chest. "In a few minutes he should be. It was probably the running and the cold air hitting his lungs that caused the reaction."

It wasn't until she finally looked up that she saw how pale the coloring was in E. C.'s face. While she was more concerned about her brother, it was obvious that E.C. was visibly shaken. He must have never been around anyone with asthma. "What about you? Are you going to be all right?'

E.C. began walking backwards, slow at first then much faster. "I...I've got to go. Take care of yourself, Aaron." He nodded to Louisa then was gone.

Anna was stunned. It almost sounded like E.C. was saying good-bye for the last time. How could he just walk away, especially now, especially from Aaron? Anna was furious with herself. This was all her fault for ever allowing him into their lives. If it was nothing more than an act of charity, why would E.C. go to the trouble? There were no extra bonus points for playing catch with a little boy.

"I hope he's not mad at me," Aaron said, his breathing much quieter and more controlled.

Anna tousled his hair. "Of course he isn't. Having asthma isn't your fault."

Aaron still looked worried. "Please don't tell Mom and Dad about this or they won't let me come back."

Anna sighed. She couldn't tell him now that she thought his playing days with E.C. were over. "If you're going to be a great football player someday we need to find out how to keep this from happening again. Come on sport, let's go home."

Louisa had remained silent until now. "He was scared, Anna."

It took a moment before Anna realized that Louisa was referring to E.C., not Aaron.

"Scared! What was I feeling and I didn't bail out?" Anna felt immediate regret for the harshness of her tone, especially in front of Aaron. But why was Louisa always defending him?

Louisa turned back around and continued washing the dishes.

"Forgive me, Louisa. I shouldn't have responded like that." Anna picked up her belongings and motioned to Aaron to leave. "I'll tell you about my weekend at All-District next Wednesday."

Anna wasn't sure if Louisa heard her over the sound of running water from the faucet, but there was no mistaking what Louisa said next.

"Remember what I told you about the crane's dance, Anna. He was once a crane, too."

Chapter Fourteen

Anna was waiting in the school van, watching the second hand on her watch make its circular pattern past each number. She was sure there must be some philosophical wisdom in observing the continual ending of one moment as a new one began, but she was more restless about how long it was taking to reach 5:00, the scheduled time for them to leave. Aside from having to share the weekend with Tonya, Anna was looking forward to the All-District clinic and performance.

The football team had already left town on its way to the game. Jessie insisted she attend the after school pep rally to watch the players load the buses, ignoring her protests that she needed to get home to finish packing. Anna made sure her presence was hidden from E.C.'s view, though that hadn't been necessary. The band and cheerleaders kept everyone's attention on them most of the time. His eyes wandered only once over the crowd as he stepped up to enter the bus, prompting her to adjust her position behind Jessie.

Anna didn't know what he was looking for, but she didn't want him to see her nonetheless.

Instead of apologizing for his abrupt exit from the center after Aaron's asthma attack, E.C. projected a new aura of indifference. He managed to destroy every positive opinion Anna had allowed her mind and her heart to create. He didn't even bother to find out how Aaron was, to make sure he was alright.

Two other orchestra members entered the van and situated themselves behind Anna's seat, Casey a viola player and John another bass player. Anna saw Kyle and Jessie outside the window saying good-bye and shook her head, wondering how they would manage to be apart from each other until Sunday. She was still disappointed Jessie wasn't going with them, but thankful she would at least have Kyle to talk to.

The only orchestra player that hadn't arrived yet was Tonya. Anna figured she was waiting until the very last moment to make her grand entrance.

"Hey," Kyle said as he entered the van. He carried his instrument to the back then sat down next to Anna.

Anna tried to scoot over to give him more room but the seats were narrow.

"It's going to be a tight fit in the van this time. Last year there were only three of us that made All-District," he remarked and then leaned across her to wave through the window.

She followed the direction of his arm and saw Jessie wave back and then link her little fingers together. Anna linked her little fingers back at Jessie. Their pinky promise had carried them through good times and bad. It was something Anna especially needed to be remembering this weekend.

"I've watched you two do that before, and as hard as I've tried, I can't get Jessie to tell me what it means." Kyle raised his eyebrows, "...but maybe I can get you to." He started swaying his duffle bag slowly in front of her. "I've got honey buns."

A wide grin spread on Anna's face. "Nothing will unseal these lips. Not even honey buns."

"Yeah, I figured as much," he laughed. "I wish we would hurry and leave, the sooner we get there the better."

Anna looked out the window again for signs of Tonya. "It appears your wish has been granted. The princess has finally arrived, and it looks like she packed for a week's vacation."

Kyle joined Anna in watching Tonya's entertaining attempt to carry a suitcase, her violin and an armload of hanging clothes. "Be glad they pair up roommates from different schools so at least you won't have to share a room with her. I bet she snores anyway, if she can part from the mirror long enough to sleep."

"I guess we'll never know. I heard her talking to Mrs. Carlson about having a single room like she did last year. She must really think she deserves special treatment," Anna said.

Kyle rubbed his fingers together. "It's all because of her daddy's money."

Their conversation was silenced as Tonya climbed in and sat right in front of Anna, placing all of her belongings on the floor and empty seat beside her.

"Talk about being stuffed in here," Tonya complained, adjusting the back of her seat and almost hitting Anna's knees.

That was all it took to spark Kyle's sarcasm. "What's wrong, your highness, not enough space for your royal wardrobe? " He leaned forward closer to her ear. "And to think, we breathe the same air."

Anna jabbed Kyle with her elbow. She had no desire to provoke Tonya. They would have to spend the next two days together in the same building and Anna didn't want to give her an extra incentive to ruin it.

Tonya didn't say anything, though her eyes shot rays of contempt.

Mrs. Carlson finally took her place in the driver's seat and the van started moving.

"I think I'll rest now while I can. Wake me up when we get there," Kyle said, leaning his head back and covering his ears with the headphones to his portable CD player.

The town hosting All-District wasn't as far away as where the auditions had been, but Anna decided to close her eyes as well. As soon as she did, random images of Louisa and the Samaritan Center began projecting in her mind like a silent movie, until one of the images caused her eyes to jerk back open. Moisture formed above her eyebrows as a flush of concern made her heart begin to beat hard and fast. Seeing Louisa dancing in the middle of a flock of cranes with one older man and another one much younger suddenly made Anna nervous about being gone from home.

It was getting darker and dimly lit silhouettes were all that could be seen through the windows. Anna glanced at Kyle wishing he was awake, but he looked too peaceful to be disturbed. She was afraid to close her eyes again.

Kyle must have felt her watchfulness. "Did you need something?" he asked, lifting off his headphones.

Anna shook her head. "Not really."

"Here listen to this, the time will pass by faster." Kyle placed the headphones over her ears before she had the chance to decline.

Within a few minutes, Anna was immersed in the soulful rhythm of jazz, feeling grateful for the diversion. Kyle was right. The time passed quickly and it wasn't long before the van had pulled up in front of the hotel.

"I didn't know you liked that kind of music," Anna said.

Kyle picked up his bag. "I listen to a lot of different kinds. It just depends on the mood I'm in."

"You two can take your time with your little conversation, but I'm getting myself out of this claustrophobic nightmare," Tonya chimed in. "You don't mind helping me, do you, Casey?"

Anna watched as the sweet venom in Tonya's voice entered its victim. As if hypnotized, Casey picked up her violin and her suitcase. Anna wanted to shake him out of his trance, but it was too late, Tonya was already leaving the van with Casey, her loyal subject, following close behind.

Heartstrings

A hair-raising tingle traveled up Anna's arm. She figured Tonya had enough ice running through her veins to cause such a chilling effect on people, but this time she knew Tonya wasn't the reason. It was the question that had plagued her ever since the audition. Was she really good enough to be here?

Once inside the hotel, Anna and Kyle joined their group in the lobby to wait for room assignments. Anna hoped she would have a nice roommate. Of some comfort was the thought that no one could be worse than Tonya.

Mrs. Carlson returned from the desk with a list and handful of keys. "Anna, you will be in room number 320," she said, extending one of the keys out to her.

As soon as the key came in contact with the palm of her hand, the moment became real. Soon she would be playing with some of the best musicians in the area. Anna wished Louisa could be there to share in this accomplishment. It was as much her victory as Anna's.

"There must be a mistake. There can't be two rooms with the number 320," Tonya blurted from across the group.

Anna's attention snapped back to the room assignments. What was Tonya talking about? Room 320 was her number.

"I'm sure it's just an error," Mrs. Carlson announced. "Everyone wait here while I see what the problem is."

Tonya held nothing back in her display of disgust with the issue. She plopped down on her suitcase with a loud huff, crossing her arms over her hanging clothes to keep them from touching the floor.

"It would appear that patience is not the prickly princess's virtue," Kyle whispered through the side of his mouth.

Anna returned a twisted smile that faded with the realization of their predicament. There was no way she would spend the night in a locked room with Tonya Sterling, and it was clear that the feeling was mutual.

The expression on Mrs. Carlson's face when she returned did nothing to dispel the growing tension. She cleared her throat and made deliberate eye contact with Tonya and Anna before speaking. "There was a mistake. Apparently there was another girl named Tonya they thought they had placed with Anna."

Tonya didn't waste any time sharing what appeared to be the obvious solution. "Well, that means the other Tonya got a room to herself, so we can just trade places."

Mrs. Carlson's voice remained smooth and calm. "That may have worked had the other Tonya not became ill this morning and had to give up her spot. The alternate in line to take her place is a boy, so trading places is not an option. Unfortunately, there are no other rooms available."

Anna heard Tonya draw in a breath as if ready to mount a verbal defense, but a sweeping glare from Mrs. Carlson challenged any further comment from the entire group. "You have thirty minutes to get settled into your rooms and meet back here for dinner. The first rehearsal begins promptly at 7:30. Are there any questions?"

If there were, no one had the nerve to speak up, not even Tonya.

Anna looked at Kyle. "I'll see you in a little while. I'm going to take the stairs up to the room."

Kyle hesitated like he should offer to go with her, but didn't. "Are you going to be okay?"

Anna nodded. It was true she wanted to stretch her legs after the cramped ride in the van, but her reason for taking the stairs instead of the elevator was more than that. She needed the few minutes alone to arm herself against Tonya's pointed remarks, determined not to become her personal pincushion.

Anna's steps slowed the closer she got to the door numbered 320. She knew Tonya was already inside. With a firm resolution, she inserted the key in the lock and opened the door.

"I hope you don't mind, I already chose the bed I wanted," Tonya said, busy unpacking her suitcase.

The bed she had chosen was the one closest to the bathroom. Other than that Anna didn't see any difference. "It doesn't matter to me."

Except for muffled voices from the hallway, the room was thick with silence, filled with the deliberate avoidance of conversation. Tonya didn't seem to want to talk, and Anna for sure didn't. Just when the awkwardness became unbearable, Tonya picked up her key and walked to the door. "I'm going ahead downstairs."

Tonya didn't wait for a response, and Anna didn't give her one. As soon as the door closed, she flung herself down on the bed with a sigh of relief. She could finally have a moment of peace. The quilted bedspread felt cool at first against her face but quickly warmed up, making Anna's tired body want to stay there and rest. Her eyes were closed until there was an unexpected knock on the door.

"Kyle's escort service is here," a voice announced.

Anna jumped up to let him in. "How did you know I was by myself?"

"I have my ways." He gave her a knowing look. "So, have you snuck around to find out what secrets she's hiding? She's bound to have some."

Anna's answer was laced with a playful but stern glare. "You know I wouldn't do that."

"I would," he said, his roving eyes already scouting out the contents of the room.

"Come on, we better leave before you do something you shouldn't." Anna took hold of Kyle's arm and guided him out the door. What she didn't need was Tonya accusing her of snooping through her belongings.

The pizza tasted good, but Anna was only able to eat one slice before apprehension over the first rehearsal claimed the rest of her appetite. It wasn't until the guest conductor led the orchestra through their opening piece of music that she began to feel more at ease. The sound from all the instruments was inspiring, slowly replacing her fears that she didn't belong there. Soon she wasn't even self-conscious about her violin or the condition of its case.

Anna hardly felt the time go by and wished they could practice all night, anything to avoid spending the rest of it alone in Tonya's presence. The one consolation was that they were probably both so tired they would go right to sleep. Besides, if earlier was any indication, Tonya didn't seem to want to talk anyway.

Kyle walked the stairs with Anna to the third floor after rehearsal and waited for her to unlock the door. "See you in the morning."

"Thanks." Anna waited until Kyle was on his way down the hall before adding, "Be sure and tell Jessie hello for me."

Kyle turned and smiled then shook his head. It shouldn't have been a surprise to him that Anna knew exactly what he planned to do next.

Anna closed and locked the door, then placed her violin on the small dresser next to the television. She did her best to ignore Tonya brushing her hair in front of the mirror and went about finding her pajamas.

"I'm hungry after all that rehearsal. Do you want something from the snack machine?" Tonya asked while getting change out of her billfold.

The unexpected question caught Anna off-guard, causing her to pause before answering, "No thanks."

"Look I'll pay for it. I've got plenty of money," she continued.

Tonya's emphasis on *plenty* was all it took to unleash Anna's defensive pride. "If I want something to eat, I'll buy it myself."

"I was just trying to be nice," Tonya struck back before leaving the room.

Anna scolded herself for playing right into Tonya's hands. That was exactly the response someone like her would get the most pleasure from. Changing into her pajamas, Anna regained her composure and vowed not to let the ice princess have that much control over her again. She was just finishing brushing her teeth when Tonya returned with a half-eaten candy bar.

"I saw that Kyle friend of yours at the vending machine. It seems like you two seem to spend a lot of time together," she said. Her eyebrows were raised with piqued interest.

So much for thinking Tonya wouldn't want to talk. It wasn't any of her business to know what their relationship was, but Anna wasn't about to let her start spreading false rumors. "Kyle is Jessie's boyfriend. If she were here it would be quite obvious."

"Oh, I was just wondering if he was that perfect person you told me about at Jake's Place." Tonya wadded up her empty candy wrapper and tossed it into the trashcan. "What do you think about E.C. Coleman? I've heard you volunteer together down at the Samaritan Center."

Tonya's question opened up a flood of emotions Anna had hoped to keep locked away for the weekend. Her mind scrambled to respond. "Why do you ask?"

"He's never had a girlfriend that I know of," she said.

E.C. was the last person Anna wanted to discuss. "That's his business. Why would it make any difference to me?"

Tonya shrugged her shoulders. "I was just going to offer you some advice in case this perfect person didn't work out for you. Many girls have tried to be his girlfriend, but no one has succeeded ...yet," she stressed with special significance.

Anna quickly realized that Tonya had every intention of being the winner of that challenge. "I suppose that's because he hasn't seen anything he's interested in...yet." She didn't intend to mimic Tonya or defend E.C. but she was fed up with Tonya's assumptions that she could have everything she desired, including E. C..

Tonya either didn't catch Anna's jab or chose to ignore its meaning. "Do you know why he chose to volunteer at the Samaritan Center?"

It was late and Anna was weary, especially with this conversation. She didn't care why E.C. chose the Samaritan Center but knew there was nothing she could do to prevent Tonya from telling her.

"It's because of his stepfather, Clarence. I bet you didn't know that Baxter Industries is a big contributor to the Samaritan Center. And since E.C. will probably follow in his stepfather's footsteps, it's important he learn all he can about the business, even the charitable side."

Anna's cheeks stung from the information that just slapped her in the face. Not only had Tonya confirmed that Clarence Baxter was E.C.'s stepfather, Baxter Industries had indirectly fed her family free meals after her father lost his job. Anna slid beneath the comfort of her bedcovers, pulling them up to her neck then turning over to face the opposite direction. She had no response to make.

"Well, I guess that means good night. Hope you don't mind my alarm going off at 5:30. I need plenty of time in the morning to get ready."

The light went off, and even though Anna was exhausted, she didn't know how she was going to fall asleep. After such an inspiring rehearsal with the orchestra, she now felt empty inside and ached from something she couldn't identify. At least she would be able to tell her mother that E.C. was for sure Charlie Coleman's son, a truth that was still impossible for her to believe.

There was also now another truth that was certain. Anna would never be able to look E.C. Coleman in the face again.

Chapter Fifteen

Tonya's alarm went off as promised at 5:30 the next morning. Anna kept her eyelids pressed together pretending not to have been awakened. Once she heard the bathroom door close, she rolled over and tried to go back to sleep. She hadn't slept very well all night, but it soon became obvious she wasn't going to get any more now. As tired as she was, the sounds coming from the shower and the anticipation of a full day of rehearsals were going to keep her awake.

Anna decided to at least stay in bed and get some rest while she waited for Tonya to come out of the bathroom. By 6:30, however, Tonya still hadn't come out, and Anna needed to go in.

She got up and knocked lightly on the door. "Are you almost finished? You've been in there for an hour."

"I told you it took me a long time to get ready. I'll be out as soon as I finish getting my make-up on," Tonya answered without a hint of apology.

"I'd appreciate it if you would please hurry," Anna muttered with diminishing restraint while she paced back and forth outside the door.

Anna's restlessness soon came from more than just necessity. She had tolerated Tonya's typical rudeness long enough and placed her hand on the doorknob. Anna was as surprised as Tonya seemed to be when the door opened, and they found themselves looking at each other eye to eye.

Tonya quickly turned away back to the mirror. "I'm not done yet."

"I can't wait until you're done. If you'll just give me a minute, you can have it all to yourself again." Anna's eyes then fell on the crowded vanity top that resembled what could have been a cosmetic company's entire product line. She had never seen so much make-up for one person. "You use all of this stuff?"

"I have to," Tonya answered, finishing applying blush across her cheeks.

Anna frowned. "That doesn't make any sense. Why would you have to?"

Tonya didn't take her eyes off her reflected image. "Because they are what it takes to look perfect."

Anna looked again at the large assortment of tubes, bottles and compacts and then back to Tonya as she continued to create her illusion of physical perfection. "That's what this is all about?"

"It's about what other people expect from me, my parents included. You have it easy. No one expects anything from you."

Anna should have been insulted, but for some reason she wasn't. Tonya's comment was laced with a thread of envy, almost sounding jealous, as ridiculous as that would be. But she was also wrong. Anna hadn't had it easy, and the suggestion that she had, caused all of her bottled-up emotions to rise up in response.

"If you never even wore make-up, you would still have the perfect face. Not to mention everything else you have that's perfect, plus Mrs. Carlson's constant attention, and a very nice violin to play. I imagine you have everything you ever wanted…everything I ever wanted." The words spewed from Anna's mouth, taking years of resentment with them.

As soon as they were gone, unexpected feelings of contentment rushed in to take their place. Anna suddenly found she no longer cared about what Tonya had. She didn't want it if unrealistic perfection was the price.

"Well, there are some days I'd give it to you," Tonya offered.

"No thank you. But you will have to excuse me now," Anna said, remembering the urgency.

Tonya left the bathroom and without turning back around said, "You know you're not such a bad violin player."

Anna started to close the door, but her newly realized confidence wouldn't let her without first responding, "Of course I'm not or I wouldn't be here."

She had never intended to discover if Tonya harbored any secrets. Unlike Kyle who was convinced that people willing to inflict misery on others were only trying to disguise what was miserable in their own lives. Anna's only desire was to have as little contact between the two of them as necessary. And with a full day of rehearsals scheduled, she got her wish. By the time they got back to their rooms that evening, it was obvious even Tonya was too exhausted to talk.

Anna couldn't remember going to sleep after her head hit the pillow. Neither did she remember hearing Tonya's alarm go off the next morning. She woke up with a start instead and looked at the clock. It was 6:30, an hour later than the previous morning. Then she looked over at the other bed, and realized Tonya must not have heard the alarm either.

Anna almost felt sorry for her, picturing how frantic she was going to be about not having enough time to get ready. She got out of bed and decided to get dressed before waking her.

"Hey, it's past time to get up. I don't think your alarm went off," she said after she was finished.

Tonya's eyes opened in response.

"The bathroom is all yours. I'm going on down to breakfast," Anna continued.

Tonya pushed the covers back and sat up. "I won't be going to breakfast."

"Suit yourself. I'll see you at rehearsal." Anna then grabbed her violin and headed out the door.

Downstairs there were trays of donuts and fruit set out with a variety of juices and hot chocolate for the orchestra members. She helped herself then found a small table to sit at and wait for Kyle. He had brought enough honey buns with him to last through the weekend so she knew he would be bringing his own breakfast.

"Don't you ever get tired of those?" Anna asked as he pulled up a chair next to her with a half-eaten one in his hand.

The sides of Kyle's mouth spread into a grin. "Never," he answered before his look became more serious. "So, how have you been surviving the prickly princess?"

Anna's eyebrows rose. "We've had our moments, but it's worked out okay."

"You must really be a saint then," he laughed.

Anna smiled. She was no saint. She just didn't think she needed to go into the details of everything that had happened between them when she wasn't sure herself. "We should probably get to rehearsal now."

Kyle and Anna went into the hall where the concert would later be performed and took their places. She couldn't help but notice when Tonya walked in and sat in a chair in the next row. It almost looked like she had waved at her.

Whether or not she had, Tonya was at least treating her with more civility. Even Kyle noticed her subdued manner the rest of the afternoon and needled Anna for answers. She didn't have any. Anna wasn't sure what had brought about the change, except that she saw Tonya in a state few others may have ever seen. A moment Tonya didn't yet look perfect.

Chapter Sixteen

Anna walked at a much faster pace toward the Samaritan Center the following Wednesday. She couldn't wait to tell Louisa how wonderful the All-District concert was, but she was also anxious to get started working on her audition pieces for Truman. Anna was finally beginning to believe she had a chance of earning a scholarship and not just because of Louisa's unwavering conviction.

At least she wouldn't have to worry about E.C. showing up to volunteer, not after his reaction to Aaron's asthma attack the week before and the distance he had kept from her since then. Louisa and Aaron may have been drawn in by his easy charm, but she should have known better. She felt worse for involving Aaron, the brother she tried so hard to protect.

Anna entered the center expecting to see Louisa waiting for her, but she wasn't. She was concerned Louisa had forgotten.

"Louisa…" Anna heard her voice travel through the empty room with an eerie hollowness.

She went first into the kitchen and then into Louisa's bedroom looking for her. Each room greeted her with the same penetrating silence. Anna wondered if Mr. Deacon had talked to Louisa and arranged for her to see a doctor. Maybe she was gone to an appointment.

Anna decided to pull out her violin and begin practicing to dispel the overwhelming quiet. She played a few scales to warm up, glancing toward the door every so often in hopes of seeing Louisa enter. When she didn't, Anna pulled out the piece Louisa had chosen for her audition. It was definitely her most challenging one yet. She was sight-reading the first page when the front door opened and Mr. Harmon walked in.

Anna immediately stopped and lowered her violin but there was no way to hide what she was doing.

"I thought I heard angels in here making music, and I see I was right. You've been keeping that special gift to yourself all this time?"

"No, Mr. Harmon." Anna shied away from his compliment. "I play in the orchestra at school and was just practicing a little."

Mr. Harmon's eyes narrowed, adding wrinkles to the ones he already wore across his forehead. "I'm no expert, but it sounded like more than a little practicing to me."

Anna looked at the clock. She had only been playing for fifteen minutes. "Why are you here so early today?"

"I thought I better check to make sure the food was here for the cooks and dinner was set to go," he answered.

Anna was surprised. "You don't ever have to do that, Mr. Harmon. Louisa always checks those things in the morning."

There was a heavy pause before he spoke again. "You don't know?"

"Know what?" Apprehension began creeping into Anna's thoughts.

"She's gone, Anna."

"I figured she had gone somewhere. Is she at an appointment or did she need to go to the store?" The words sprung from her mouth all at once, imploring Mr. Harmon to provide her with a reasonable explanation.

Mr. Harmon put his head down for a moment then looked back up. "No, Anna, she's gone for good...gone on to a better place."

Anna stared at him like he must have lost his senses. "What are you talking about? Louisa doesn't have anywhere else to go. Besides, she wouldn't leave without saying good-bye. She wouldn't leave...me..."

Her eyes widened as she translated the seriousness emanating from Mr. Harmon's face. "No, it can't be true," she said, taking a step back.

"Louisa passed away, Anna. Mr. Deacon came to check on her Monday morning and found her in her room."

Anna shook her head. "No!"

The concern in Mr. Harmon's eyes grew. "We'll all miss her, Anna."

Miss her! The words struck Anna with all their inadequacy, but of course he wouldn't understand. No one would. "What about a funeral?" Anna asked as she struggled to stay composed.

Mr. Harmon's answer was soft. "There won't be one as far as I know. You know she didn't have any family or anybody close to her."

"...*I have you...*" Louisa said to her that Sunday afternoon at the park while they sat on the bench. "...*I have you...*"

The haunting echo produced a sickening swell of nausea, and her body began to sway. She had to leave before her legs buckled beneath her. Without another word, she turned and ran out of the building.

Tears blurred Anna's vision as she moved with an uncontrollable will toward the park. Numb to her surroundings, she finally came to rest on the same wooden park bench that Louisa had brought her to. Despair poured out of her without restraint. Anna laid her head on the spot where Louisa had sat and continued to sob until exhaustion took over and her thoughts became surreal, detached from the reality she couldn't accept. It was the only place she felt at peace and protected from the truth, a place she never wanted to leave.

She didn't know how much time had passed when she sensed the slight pressure of a hand touching her shoulder, but it wasn't enough to draw her out of the refuge she had created for herself.

"Anna."

The beckoning voice sounded very far away, though it was familiar to her. When she tried to open her mouth to answer, she couldn't.

"Anna."

This time the voice sounded more desperate and she felt her body being lifted to a sitting position. The swollen lids of her eyes parted to see the figure holding her up. As soon as Anna saw that it was E.C. she covered her face with her hands. "What are you doing here?"

E.C. loosened his grip. "Mr. Harmon was worried about you and asked for my help. Now I know why. It was sheer luck that I drove by the park and saw you here."

"Well, you can inform Mr. Harmon that you found me, and go on back to your life. I'm all right."

"You're not all right, Anna. I have no intention of leaving you here like this."

Anna dropped her hands to glare at him. "You didn't have any trouble leaving when Aaron had his asthma attack," she lashed out then looked away.

E.C. sat on the bench beside her then turned her chin so she would have to look at him. "I came to the Samaritan Center today to apologize. I never should have left you and Aaron like that. I'm sorry, and I'm sorry about Louisa."

The pain was too fresh, and Anna couldn't stop a new flow of tears at the mention of her friend and mentor's name. In the next moment her face was pressed against E.C.'s shoulder and his arms were gently wrapped around her. She couldn't sort through her feelings fast enough to resist his offer of comfort, and for now it didn't matter. Anna was warm and calm; lulled by the steady rhythm of the strong pulse she felt beating from his neck.

"I'd like to take you home. Then I could apologize to Aaron as well," he said, breaking the delicate quiet.

E.C.'s statement forced Anna to reach through her stupor of grief and take hold of the present. This was the same boy that had ignored her existence for the past week and was volunteering at the Samaritan Center, not just to ensure a good grade, but to gain access into the charities his stepfather's business supported. She didn't want to go home, nor would she let him take her anyway.

Anna pulled herself away. "I don't want to go yet."

"It won't do you any good to stay here." E.C. hesitated then added slowly, "I know Louisa was a nice woman, but is there another reason why you're so upset?"

"You wouldn't understand."

"I would if you would give me a chance."

"What's to keep you from running off again?" Anna's skepticism demanded.

E.C. held his mouth firm before he finally responded in a voice barely above a whisper. "I've told you I'm sorry."

Anna wanted to trust him, but she was too confused. "I don't know what to believe anymore."

"Maybe someday you'll believe me." E.C. stood up from the bench. "In the meantime, may I please take you home?"

Anna closed her eyes and shook her head. When she opened them again he was gone. She heard an engine start and saw the passing movement of his blue Camaro as he drove off. Louisa had told her she could feel all her blessings from this bench, yet right now all Anna felt was the throbbing in her head and the cold shifting wind. The numbness had almost worn off and she was alone, staring at the pond.

The ducks kept Anna mesmerized until a honk drew her attention away, and she saw Jessie's car stop. Jessie was soon running toward her.

"Anna..." Jessie took one look at her and gathered her into a hug.

Anna's voice cracked. "This is my fault because I should have gotten help to Louisa sooner. I didn't want anything to be wrong with her, and sometimes she did seem just fine. What am I going to do, Jessie?"

Jessie took Anna by the shoulders and gave her a stern look. "This is not your fault, Anna Holmes. I'm sure Louisa knew she was sick and would have gotten help if she wanted it. She was ready to go."

"But I wasn't ready for her to go," Anna blurted out, wiping newly formed moisture from her eyes. "I still need her."

"You'll always have her, in everything she ever taught you. You're going to make her prouder than I know she already was."

Anna's mind spun in its attempt to recreate her lessons with Louisa. Nothing happened. "I don't remember anything."

"Of course you don't now, but you will. I promise," Jessie insisted.

"Mr. Harmon said there wasn't even going to be a funeral." Anna turned to Jessie. "Is that what happens to people who die who have no family...? Are they just to be forgotten about?"

"I don't have those answers, Anna, but I know Louisa will never be forgotten. Look at how your life changed because of her." Jessie helped her to her feet. "Come on, I've got to get you out of this cold air before you catch pneumonia."

They were halfway to the car when Anna stopped Jessie. "Wait, how did you know about Louisa and where to find me?"

Jessie looked into Anna's inquiring eyes. "E.C. came to my house and told me. He was worried, and knew you would let me take you home."

"E.C. came to your house?"

"Yes he did. Listen, Anna, I don't know him very well, but I'm good at telling whether or not someone is sincere or bluffing. No matter what your opinion is of him, he cared about what happened to you today."

Anna and Jessie were silent on the drive to the café, each one occupied by their own thoughts. "Your parents already know about Louisa," Jessie said once they pulled up in front of the door. "Your violin and books should be home now, too."

"Thanks, Jessie."

Jessie gave her the beginning of a smile. "I'll talk to you tomorrow."

Anna nodded and went inside. Her parents were sympathetic, but like everyone else, they had no idea how important Louisa had been in her life. After climbing the stairs to her room, she started to reach for a comb off the dresser and saw the large white envelope from Truman sitting on the corner. Her hands trembled as she picked it up instead. With Louisa gone, there was no reason to keep the application. There would be no audition.

In a matter of a few steps, Anna stood over her trash can and threw the envelope…and her dream away.

Chapter Seventeen

For the past week Anna had been forced to think and move against her will, especially during orchestra class. Her fingers could barely clasp the bow to play her violin, despite Mrs. Carlson's encouraging glances toward her. Wednesday had come again too soon. She wasn't sure she was ready to go back to the Samaritan Center yet, but she knew they needed her help.

"Since this is the last week for the extra credit assignment, the due date for your essays will be a week from this Friday," Mr. Jenkins announced, creating a ripple of groans. "That should still give those of you who haven't started yet plenty of time."

Mr. Jenkins then walked from his desk to the front of the classroom with a sheet of paper in his hand. "I do have one already turned that I'd like to share with you, though I'll keep the author's name anonymous."

Mr. Jenkins' words fed into Anna's despondent mind in slow motion. She was thankful he hadn't required her to write one.

"Instead of a traditional essay format, this one is written as a poem, so you may need to listen more carefully," he added.

Anna's curiosity was roused just enough to look at Mr. Jenkins and attempt to follow along as he began reading:

They stand and form a single line,
Accepting food on which to dine.
Their numbers count more than a few,
Igniting fear, one could be you.

I didn't want to know their name,
Where they'd been or why they came
I was there to serve a meal,
Rejecting all that seemed too real.

Most of them accept their fate,
Especially those whose hour grows late.
Though given little, if any choice,
No bitterness resides within their voice.

Sometimes it takes another's eyes,
To strip the veil of man's disguise.
Only then was it revealed to me,
Who it was I was meant to be.

After Mr. Jenkins finished, Anna saw the heads of her classmates turn and look at the people around them as if that would identify the author of the poem. It sounded like the community service assignment had opened up at least one person's eyes to the harsher realities of life.

The words "single line" and "dine" stuck in Anna's thoughts. She glanced at E.C. who was sitting still and quiet, but knew he wouldn't have written the poem. The Samaritan Center wasn't the only place in town that provided meals for the needy. Unfortunately, E.C. caught Anna's gaze before she could avert her eyes, sealing the moment with uncertainty when neither one turned away. The memory of being in his arms at the park came flooding back and she almost blushed.

Mr. Jenkins' loud voice broke through their silent communication, steering everyone's eyes back to him. "I hope some of you will continue doing volunteer work on your own. The experience can be as rewarding for the giver, if not more so, than the receiver."

"We do have one more important topic to discuss before the end of class. Anyone care to predict the score for Friday's play-off game?"

A round of spontaneous guessing pursued before Mr. Jenkins prompted E.C. "What does our quarterback think?"

E.C. didn't seem to recognize himself as the object of the question but finally answered. "28 to 10, Madison wins."

There was something missing in his answer. The words were there but his usual arrogance wasn't. She was too tired to wonder why, too tired from the sleep that kept eluding her at night, and too tired from being forced to maintain her normal routine as if nothing had changed.

Anna had heard the football team was having extended practices to prepare for the game, so E.C. wouldn't be volunteering this last week even if he wanted to. It was just as well. Aaron was home from school with a cold and wouldn't be able to play catch this afternoon anyway.

When the bell rang, Anna waited for most of the class to leave before she got up from her desk. She didn't need to hurry since there wasn't a violin lesson to get to. What she didn't expect was to see E.C. leaning against the lockers just outside the doorway. There was no way to avoid walking right by him.

He stepped in front of her to stop her. "Anna, I wanted you to know I'd be at the center today if it weren't for the play-offs. Would you please tell Aaron I'll catch him later?"

All Anna could do to respond was nod her head. E.C. checked the time on his watch and started moving backwards. "I've got to get to practice, but I hope I'll see you and Aaron at the game Friday night."

E.C. turned and ran before Anna could give him her excuse for not going. She had already told Jessie she couldn't because the café might be extra busy that night with the big game being played in town. Her parents would need her help.

Anna watched E.C. hurry down the hallway and saw Tonya wave to him to get his attention. He barely acknowledged her attempt, making Anna almost feel sorry for her. She had a feeling E.C. was one prize Tonya wasn't going to win.

Once outside, Anna started walking in the direction of the Samaritan Center. The closer she came to the building, the heavier her legs felt and the harder it was to pick up her feet. It had only been a week since her world was turned upside down by the loss of her friend and teacher. While Anna had begun to accept Louisa's death, nothing could shake her out of her apathy. She couldn't figure out how to continue playing the violin without her. Worse yet, she didn't want to.

Anna came face to face with the wooden door and hesitated. She knew there was no longer a small, white-haired woman with eyes that seemed to transcend invisible barriers waiting for her. In some way, though, Anna hoped her presence would still be felt.

With a deep breath Anna entered the room and saw Mr. Harmon putting out extra chairs. She slowly exhaled, "Hi, Mr. Harmon."

Her unexpected voice caused him to knock one over. "Miss Anna! I wasn't sure if you were coming today, but I'm glad you're here," he said, bending down to pick it up.

Anna tried to smile. "Thanks. I didn't mean to startle you." Her eyes wandered around the room checking to see if everything was the same except for Louisa's absence.

"You know I was worried about you last week. I hardly got to ask that football player to find you before he dashed out of here. If it weren't for him…" Mr. Harmon finished the sentence by shaking his head.

The reference to E.C. made her think of his words to her after school. He said he hoped to see her and Aaron at the game, but how could he when he was busy on the field. Anna's feelings were the most confused they had ever been. Maybe he did really care about them. Even if he did, though, the uncertainty of how he would react to the truth of her family's circumstances was too great. She didn't want anyone's pity, especially his.

Anna looked at Mr. Harmon and saw the distress still evident in his eyes. She walked over to him and took hold of one of his hands. Its worn surface was rough but tender. "You're a good friend, Mr. Harmon. I don't know what I'd do without you."

Mr. Harmon's dark brown eyes softened.

"I'm going to walk around for a few minutes, and then I'll be back to help you," she said then released his hand.

Anna went to the kitchen first, her mind holding fast to an image of Louisa standing at the sink with soap suds up to her elbows. She closed her eyes and listened to the stillness, hoping the walls would release the sounds of Louisa's singing they must have absorbed over time. Instead, only the hum from the refrigerator and an occasional drip of water from the faucet could be heard.

She then moved on to Louisa's bedroom and was taken aback by its sterile appearance. There was no visible evidence of anyone having occupied the room.

The bed was stripped of its covers and the shelves were completely emptied. Anna searched for some reminder of Louisa, something left behind she could take with her.

Her eyes followed a path to the desk and stopped. Anna walked over to it and pulled open the top drawer. Inside was Louisa's comb, the one she had used on Louisa's hair the day she was expecting Felix to visit her. Anna picked it up and ran her thumb over its teeth. If Louisa and Milo did have a son named Felix that died fighting for Hungary's freedom, they were all reunited now. She slipped the comb in her coat pocket and after one more contemplative search, left the room.

Mr. Harmon watched her return but looked reticent to say anymore.

"I'll be all right, Mr. Harmon," Anna reassured him. "It's just going to take time to get used to her not being here." She started to go back into the kitchen to get the trays.

"I found out where she's buried," he said, causing her to pause. "Mr. Deacon told me she's at the Memorial Lane Cemetery. Apparently, she purchased a plot some time ago."

Anna turned to look at Mr. Harmon. His face was apprehensive. "Thank you, Mr. Harmon. I'm glad you told me." She took in a breath of thanksgiving. Louisa must have taken care of her own arrangements when Milo died. The thought of them buried beside each other gave her a small amount of peace.

It wasn't long after Anna took her place alone in the serving line, that she realized how much help E.C.

had been to her. One of the cooks came over to assist her, but with the volunteer assignment over, Anna knew she better get used to managing by herself again.

She heard Mr. Harmon whistling as he came in right away to start washing dishes. No longer hearing Louisa's songs was more painful than she thought it would be. "If you don't mind, as soon as I get the containers emptied, I think I'll go home."

"You go on right now; I'll take care of everything," he insisted.

Anna hesitated at first, feeling guilty for leaving more work for Mr. Harmon, but with his urging, she gave in, silently vowing to make it up to him next time.

She had been keeping her violin at school so she only had to grab her books and jacket to go home. She planned to visit the cemetery as soon as she could, but this evening she was anxious to see how Aaron was feeling, hoping his cold was better.

After greeting her parents Anna ran up the stairs and found her brother looking at one of his books.

"What are you doing?" she asked, bouncing onto his bed.

Aaron sniffled. "Looking at the pictures."

"We could read a book together." Anna went to his bookshelf and fingered through his books, pulling out, *The Little Engine That Could*.

Aaron frowned when he saw his sister's choice. "That's a baby book."

Anna paused to look at its cover then opened the book and began flipping through the pages. "I'm just trying to remember how the story goes."

Aaron wiped his nose then reminded her. "It's about the little blue engine that climbed the mountain by saying, 'I think I can, I think I can.'"

Tears threatened to fill the rim of Anna's eyelids as she read the words at the same time. Had Louisa known the story, she would have constantly reminded Anna to think just like the little blue engine had.

"Are you okay?" Aaron asked.

"Yeah, I'm fine." She closed the book, but as she did, something caught her eye. Anna opened the cover to look again. Coleman's Bookstore was stamped in black ink on the inside. A strange sensation pulsed through her fingers at the thought that she was touching something E.C.'s father may have touched. She carefully placed the book back on the shelf.

"E.C. told me that he couldn't come to the Samaritan Center today because of the extra football practice but that he'd catch you later. I didn't get a chance to tell him that you were sick and couldn't be there anyway."

"Good, I don't want him to think I'm some kind of sissy." Aaron picked up his yo-yo and wound the string.

Anna gave him a stern glare. "No one better ever think that about my brother." She forced a smile. "Do you still want to read something?"

"Maybe later," he answered, watching his yo-yo spin down and back up.

"Then I'm going to the kitchen to see if Mom and Dad need help." Anna took the steps two at a time and found her mother scrubbing the grill. "You mentioned going inside Coleman's Bookstore, but you never mentioned buying any books there."

Her mother's face grew with perplexity.

"The Little Engine That Could," Anna prompted.

"Oh, yes, of course," she answered. "You were very young when Mr. Coleman convinced me that every child should own the book about the little blue engine. I must have read it to you hundreds of time. Do you remember?"

Anna nodded that she did, musing still about the book's simple message of willingness and perseverance. A lesson not just for "babies" as Aaron had said.

"There you are, Anna." her father said, entering the kitchen with a tray of pie crusts ready to be filled. "I've been meaning to talk to you about the pies."

"I'm sorry if they haven't been as good lately…it's been hard since…"

"No, Anna, you misunderstand," he interrupted. "They have become very popular. I sell out of them almost every day and have to make extra after the lunch crowd dies down. I hate to ask you to bake more but we've had some disappointed customers, and I don't think mine are near as good as yours."

The lines between his eyebrows suddenly became more pronounced. "It's interesting, too, that we keep running out of the butterscotch. For the past few weeks a gentleman has been coming in around 11:00 every Monday to buy a whole pie. He never says much, just hands me a twenty dollar bill and leaves. I tried to give him his change the first time, but he wouldn't take it."

The night E.C.'s mother ordered the piece of butterscotch pie rose to the surface of Anna's memory. She could still picture Mrs. Baxter's face as she remarked how good it was. Anna wondered if it was possible for the two incidences to be related then quickly shrugged off the idea.

"I'll try to make some more butterscotch then at least," Anna offered.

"Dad…" she started to continue, unsure how to word the question that refused to go unanswered any longer.

"Yes, Anna."

"Weren't you angry when you lost your job at Baxter Industries?"

The shock and unexpected timing of her question was immediately apparent. Her parents sent looks of bewilderment toward each other before facing her again.

Her mother was the first to speak. "What makes you ask this now, Anna? That part of our life was so long ago."

Anna didn't answer, waiting to hear her father's response first. Both confusion and concern were molded into his face.

"Angry…no, Anna, we were never angry. The whole town was hurting. A little worried, yes, but in the end we felt like we were the lucky ones."

"Lucky? We lost our home and had to depend on charity to eat! How can you use the word 'lucky'?"

Anna's father crossed his arms as he appeared to be choosing his next words more carefully. "We were lucky in that we were able to stay here. Some people had to leave town to find other jobs. I didn't want to move my family and risk making things more difficult than they already were. And it was Baxter Industries that made it possible for us to open the café."

Anna sat on a nearby stool and rested her head. She wouldn't be able to fight off her exhaustion much longer. "What would Baxter Industries have to do with a family owned café?"

This time Mrs. Holmes answered. "They allowed us to borrow from the company's retirement fund to get started. By the time they offered your father his job back we had already invested too much of ourselves and our money to accept."

As soon as her mother's words sunk in, Anna sat straight up and looked directly at her father. She couldn't believe what she had just heard. "You could have had a real job again and you didn't take it? You both work so hard all the time and we still struggle."

Anna saw how the sharpness in her voice affected him. "I'm sorry...I just don't understand."

"I'm sorry, too, Anna. I didn't think it mattered that you knew. The cafe hasn't seemed so much like hard work. I enjoy providing a place where people can get good food and good service."

Anna's emotions simmered with conflict as she sought to make sense of this new information. His words were laced with such pride, something she had never recognized in him, or couldn't, because of her own self-imposed embarrassment of their circumstances.

Her father's eyes suddenly filled with alarm. "I regret that money has been scarce, but I hope our decision hasn't made your life unhappy. For that, I could never forgive myself."

Whatever she was feeling, Anna didn't want her father to feel guilty for a decision he thought was best for all of them. She put her arms around his neck and hugged him close.

After a few moments he pulled back and smiled. "The loan is paid off now, so we can help you get a new violin and maybe some lessons before your audition at the university."

Anna wanted to return his smile but she couldn't. She didn't have the heart to tell him that, now, was too late. There would be no audition.

Chapter Eighteen

A glow from the street lamp filtered through the windows of the café, casting long shadows across the floor. The last group of customers had just left, and Anna was now pushing a broom around each table, determined to get the job done as quickly as possible. She didn't dare sit down for a moment's rest for fear she wouldn't get back up. While the extra business from the playoff game was welcome, her feet and back were throbbing in protest.

It didn't help that she spent the afternoon after school walking through row after row of the cemetery searching for Louisa's grave. When Anna finally found the small white cross bearing the name, Louisa Kovack, she stopped and shuddered. Looking beside it she saw the tombstone with the inscription, Milo Kovack, 1906-1971.

"Louisa and Milo Kovack," Anna said, rolling the words over in her mouth. Seeing their names beside each other gave her a small amount of closure, but the ache in her chest was still there. Leaving the cemetery, she wondered if the hurt would ever go away.

Anna knew she had made the right decision to stay home from the game. Even when her mother encouraged her to leave and join Jessie at halftime, she didn't. It would have been too difficult for her parents to manage the cafe by themselves, and by the weight of her pockets, she would have missed out on a generous amount of tips. At least Aaron had recovered enough from his cold to go.

Glancing at the time on the clock, Anna realized the game must be over. She wished she could find out who won, but Aaron was spending the night with a friend and wouldn't be home until the next day. It looked like she would have to wait to find out if Madison won the playoffs.

Anna paused long enough to tuck a stray hair behind her ear and survey the last section of floor to be swept. She gripped the broom's handle and began to push again when the bell on the front door rang. Her head whipped around as she jumped.

"Sorry, I hope I didn't scare you."

Anna stared at the silhouetted figure standing before her while her heart drummed heavily against the wall of her chest. "You just surprised me. I guess I forgot to lock the door… and turn the sign around," she said after noticing that "Closed" was still facing the inside of the café."

E.C. stepped in closer. "I asked Jessie where you were when I didn't see you at the game."

Anna didn't understand how he could have talked to Jessie, but the seriousness on his face pulled her thoughts back to the outcome of the playoffs. She barely had the courage to ask. "Did we win?"

He nodded his head. "Yeah, but it wasn't because of me. Let's just leave it that I couldn't have played much worse."

Anna was relieved they had won, but her legs couldn't bear her weight any longer and she sat down on the closest barstool. "We all have our days when nothing seems to go right. I'm sure Aaron and all your other fans will still think you're the greatest."

He looked down before meeting her gaze in silence.

Anna swiveled back and forth on the stool to combat her increasing self-consciousness. This was the most they had talked since Louisa died. "Everyone must be out celebrating."

E.C. nodded. "Probably at Jakes, but I wanted to see you instead."

If Anna was mystified by his unexpected appearance, she was even more so now by his desire to be with her rather than celebrate winning the district playoffs with the rest of the football team. She was too puzzled to respond.

"There's something I'd like to show you. Can you leave to take a walk?" he asked.

Anna felt trapped. She couldn't leave without telling her parents. But how could she without him figuring out that her parents were upstairs, and that the café was her home? Her mouth tried to form an answer.

"It's okay, Anna, I know you live here over the café and that you would need to ask your parents." E.C.'s voice was void of any judgment.

Anna closed her eyes then opened them to face the truth. "How long have you known?"

"For a little while," he answered.

She cringed at all her foolish attempts to keep it from him. "It must not seem like much of a home to you."

E.C. sat down on the barstool next to her. "On the contrary, what could be better than smelling great food cooking all day? Though I think I'd always be hungry."

Anna relaxed enough to smile. "You get used to the all smells. Sometimes it even ruins my appetite. I mean...don't get me wrong, the food is great, but day after day..."

"Anna," he smiled back, "how about that walk?"

Anna hoped she hadn't been rambling. She often did when she felt nervous. Maybe it was because this was the closest they had been to each other since he held her on the bench at the park. "Sure, just let me tell my parents and get the key."

When she returned, E.C. opened the door and they stepped outside. He paused to turn and face her. "The first thing I want to do is apologize for the day you found out Louisa died."

Anna opened her mouth to dispute the need for an apology when his hand came close to her lips to stop her.

"If I said or did anything wrong at the park, I'm sorry. It's haunted me every day since then that you didn't trust me enough to take you home. I know I've disappointed you but I'm hoping after tonight you'll understand."

In Anna's hurry to leave the café, she had forgotten that it was November and that she should have at least grabbed a sweater to wear. She locked her arms tightly together to protect herself from the chilly air.

"Here, put this on." E.C. took off his jacket and held it for her to put on. "We just have a couple of blocks to walk."

Anna didn't have time to hesitate and put her arms into its sleeves. She felt like she had entered a warm oven from the body heat still infused in the lining of the wool and leather jacket. Her goose bumps immediately subsided at the same time her senses became acutely aware of a familiar scent. Turning her nose toward her shoulder, the scent became stronger and she realized where she had smelled it before. It was in the park when E.C. held her on the bench. He must have been wearing this jacket or something else that smelled of the same cologne.

"Thank you." Anna followed beside E.C., struggling with the awkwardness of wearing something too big for her and the uncertainty of where they were going. She dared to glance over at him and found him looking up at the sky. Her eyes followed his line of vision. The clear night gave the moon and the stars with all their constellations a solid, dark palette to shine from.

Anna was still looking at the stars when E.C. stopped in front of one of the stores. "We're here."

She found herself scanning the familiar features of the store she frequently visited on errands for the cafe. "Waite's Hardware Store?" she asked with increasing confusion.

"It hasn't always been a hardware store." He looked squarely at Anna before he continued. "Have you ever heard of Coleman's Bookstore?"

A shiver of anticipation ran through her veins despite the warmth generated from E.C's jacket. "Yes, I have."

"That was my father's store. He loved books and was always ordering more than he could fit on the shelves. I remember once suggesting that he get a bigger place. He only smiled at me and said he didn't want to take the chance of losing the magic. I never really understood what he meant until he was gone." E.C. was quiet for the next few moments. "You can tell me if you don't want to hear anymore."

"No, please go on. I'd like to know more about him," Anna gently urged.

E.C. sat on the steps and Anna joined him. "There isn't a whole lot more to tell. His name was Charles, like my middle name, though everyone called him Charlie. Besides loving books, he also was a great piano player. In the evenings after dinner, he would sit down to play, and then have me sit on the bench next to him so he could teach me something before I had to go to bed."

"So, you do know how to play the piano," Anna said more to herself as she remembered what her mother had told her.

"It's been a long time since I've touched one. I was afraid hearing the music would make my mother sad. At first I tried practicing when she wasn't home, so I wouldn't forget what he had taught me. But once the store closed and my mother remarried, everything changed. That was when the magic and the music in my life ended."

Anna already knew that E.C. was the son of Charlie Coleman from what Tonya had told her, but the knowledge of what else her mother said about the family came rushing back. She swallowed hard. "You had a little brother, didn't you?"

E.C. looked questioningly at Anna before answering. "Not for very long. He died a few months after he was born." He picked up a fallen leaf by his foot and began tearing it into small pieces. "I had made big plans for the two of us."

"I'm so sorry." The words sounded incredibly inadequate to Anna as selfish guilt settled over her. She had been so caught up in her own life and in her own pain; she didn't think about anyone else's. "What happened to him?"

E.C. threw the last remnant of leaf on the ground. "I don't think they know for sure. My father went to check on him one afternoon while he was asleep in his crib and found he had quit breathing. It wasn't even six months after Aaron died, when my father died from a heart attack. By the age of eleven, I had lost half of my family."

Anna's throat went dry and she could scarcely find her tongue to speak. "Aaron, was your brother's name?" As each word left her mouth, the dizzying reality of why E.C. reacted like he had toward her brother was obvious.

"Maybe now you'll understand why I didn't handle myself very well when your brother's asthma acted up and he started wheezing. The thought of losing someone else I had come to care about so much about was terrifying, especially someone with the same name."

Hearing E.C. tell this compelling piece of information cast everything in a different light. "I had no idea…" The rest of Anna's sentence was lost as she realized she hadn't suffered near the loss he had. She was the one who should be sorry.

"Sometime life seems so unfair," she added after a moment.

The side of E.C.'s mouth lifted in a partial grin. "I'll ask you the same two questions my father used to ask me." He then looked at Anna. "Would you eat a lion?"

Anna responded with an amused frown. "Of course not."

E.C.'s face then broke into a full grin. "Would a lion eat you?"

"Yes," she chuckled.

"See, life is unfair." E.C. kept his gaze steady on her. "But my father also told me things have a way of working out if you can keep from being afraid."

Anna felt like she was seeing a different person in front of her. That is, except for those same extraordinary eyelashes.

"I wish I had your eyelashes," she said, feeling a new boldness.

"Well, if I could, I'd be happy to give them to you," he laughed.

"It wouldn't take much to help these boring eyes of mine." Anna laughed easily along with him, realizing how long it had been and how good it felt.

She started to look away but was drawn back by E.C's next statement.

"You're wrong you know. Your eyes are far from boring." E.C. caught her attention before he continued. "I can see everything that you love in them. I see how much you care about what you do and about the people around you."

Anna was wrapped up in his comment, unable to break the silence that followed.

"It's late. I better walk you home now." E. C. stood up to leave.

They had taken a few steps when she found her voice again, "Thank you for bringing me here."

E.C. paused to look at her. "I should be the one thanking you."

Anna was puzzled. "For what?"

"Sometimes it takes another's eyes, to strip the veil of man's disguise," he answered.

She stopped and fixed her eyes directly on him. "That was your poem?"

"Doesn't fit the quarterback image very well, does it?" E.C. remarked before his expression became serious again. "I want to tell you something else before I lose the courage."

He looked away and then back again. "There's something different about you. You're the first girl I've felt like I could be myself around."

The palms of Anna's hands were wet with perspiration, but it wasn't because of the warmth of the pockets of E.C.'s jacket. Her next words felt jumbled as she spoke. "I'm glad. I feel terrible I was so hard on you in the beginning."

"I have to admit you were a little scary when I first met you," E.C. teased.

Anna held back an impatient giggle. "I shouldn't have forced you to wear those awful gloves that really were too small."

The visual created from those words brought unrestrained laughter from both of them that lasted the remaining distance back to the café.

Anna pulled the key out of her pocket and inserted it into the lock. "If you don't have plans tomorrow afternoon, you could come by if you want. I know Aaron would be excited to see you."

"I'll see you tomorrow then," E.C. answered, beginning to back up slowly toward his car.

Anna watched him open the driver's door. "How did you know I wasn't at the game tonight?"

E.C.'s chin tilted with a sly smile. "Section C, fifth row up," he answered before getting in.

Anna couldn't believe he had noticed. She pushed against the café door to open it when she felt the cushion of E.C.'s jacket against her arm. "Wait!" she hollered to get his attention again, but he was already driving away.

Once inside, Anna quietly climbed the stairs to her bedroom, reflecting on the evening with each step. Something special had happened tonight. Her mind replayed their conversation and she heard his words again, "You're the first girl I've felt like I could be myself...." Everything he told her was because he trusted her. It was her turn now to show she trusted him. It was time for her to quit being afraid.

Anna already felt lighter from her realization. She went into Aaron's room and studied its contents draped in the moonlight. His car collection on the shelf, the posters on the wall, and the football on his nightstand took on a greater significance. He wasn't asleep in his bed tonight, but he would be tomorrow, unlike E.C.'s little brother. She had wasted years dwelling on the things she thought she didn't have when all along she had what mattered most. Like her father said, they were "lucky."

She slipped off E. C.'s jacket and laid it out on Aaron's bedspread where he would soon find it. If only for a little while, he could pretend like he was E.C. Coleman, star quarterback of the Madison High football team.

Chapter Nineteen

"Wow!"

Anna heard Aaron's exclamation from the base of the stairs. She had been waiting all morning for her brother to get home and hear what his reaction would be as soon as he entered his room. In the next instant he was leaping down the steps toward her holding onto E.C.'s jacket.

"Try it on," Anna said.

Aaron looked at the jacket and then back at Anna.

"It's okay, I promise," she assured him.

Aaron slipped each arm through the leather sleeves and stood as tall as he could. "It almost fits."

Anna noticed his fingertips were barely visible but was careful not to hurt his pride. "You're right it does, though you'll have to give it back this afternoon when E.C. comes by."

"E.C.'s coming here…today?"

Anna nodded.

"Yes!" Aaron swung his fist in front of him.

"I heard he didn't play very well at the game last night," Anna probed, curious about her brother's opinion.

Aaron shrugged his shoulders. "It's okay, we're still going to the state playoffs," he answered while pretending to launch a football down the hallway.

"Maybe you should go outside and warm-up a little in case E.C. wants to play catch." Anna watched as her suggestion spread anticipation across Aaron's face. "I bet you won't even have to ask him."

Aaron ran out the door reminding Anna how he always seemed to handle life with a greater ease than she ever had, even with his asthma always poised to strike. She went into the kitchen and found her mother stacking the clean plates from lunch.

"It's true, Mom," she said, stepping in to place them back on the shelf.

Her mother gave her a curious smile. "What is?"

"That E.C. Coleman is Charlie Coleman's son. The 'C' in his initials stands for Charles, after his father."

Mrs. Holmes's smile turned thoughtful. "I knew there was something familiar about him the day he brought your violin and notebook home. His eyes were so gentle, just like I remember Mr. Coleman's."

Anna let her mother's words sink in. That was what she had detected in E.C.'s eyes the night she waited on him and his mother at the café. It was gentleness. She couldn't see it when he first came to volunteer at the Samaritan Center. Her defenses had already judged and sentenced him before she knew anything about the person inside. Yet he had always been gentle with Aaron and with her when she would let him.

She started to tell her mother that he was coming by this afternoon, but she didn't get the chance. As soon as the bell clanged against the door Mrs. Holmes left the kitchen to greet the potential customer.

"Why hello, E.C. It's good to see you again." Anna heard her mother say on the other side of the swinging door.

"Hi, Mrs. Holmes, how are you?" returned his deep voice.

Anna left the kitchen to join them.

E.C. smiled at her appearance. "Hi, Anna."

Anna's mother glanced from one to the other before asking E.C., "Can I get you something to eat?"

"No, thank you. I only came by to see Anna and Aaron if this is a good time."

"Of course, though had we been busy like last night, I just might have put an apron on you. How are you at peeling potatoes?" her mother teased.

"I would have been glad to help, Mrs. Holmes. I've gotten to know my way around the kitchen pretty well," he added with the words directed straight toward Anna.

"Be careful or I might take you up on that." Her mother laughed then continued in a more wistful tone, "I do miss your father's bookstore. I was so sorry to hear when he passed away. There was something so peaceful and inspiring about being surrounded by all of those books. It was a place where you could spend hours and never realize it, like time stood still."

"Yes, it was." E.C.'s attention was drawn away for a moment as his eyes became fixed on the café's windows. "When I was little I used to get into trouble for climbing on the ladder wanting to see all those books, especially the ones on the top shelf." His attention returned to Anna and her mother. "I think we still have every book that was left."

"I always wondered what happened to all of them," Anna's mother remarked. "The store closed so quickly."

"I think they're all still in boxes in our attic," E.C. answered. "I found them one afternoon while I was exploring Mr. Baxter's house after we moved in. I don't know if my mother even remembers we have them."

Anna listened to this exchange between her mother and E.C. noting how comfortable he appeared to be talking about a past that she knew had more scars than her own. She wondered how many of his friends knew about them.

"Well, I better get back to work in the kitchen. If you get hungry, let me know." Anna's mother offered before she walked away and disappeared behind the door.

E.C. waited until the thumping of its hinges stopped. "Your mother is very nice."

"So, is yours," Anna said, recollecting the night she took Mrs. Baxter's order. His mother had been polite and gracious, even through the awkwardness of calling her by what she knew now to be the wrong last name.

"Unfortunately, there are some things my mother and I quit talking about. It's good to know someone remembers my father and his bookstore," he said.

Anna was trying to figure out something reassuring to say to him when the front door burst open.

"I knew I saw your car drive by," Aaron said, running into the cafe.

E.C. threw his head back at the sight of Anna's brother wearing his letterman jacket that hung halfway to his knees and almost past his fingers.

Anna worried when a pale expression took over E.C.'s face, the same expression he got in the center the day Aaron had his asthma attack. "I didn't think you would mind if Aaron wore your jacket for awhile today since you forgot it last night.

"I tried to catch you before you drove off to give it back to you," she hurried to add.

"I forgot I had left it," he said, shaking his head. "Hey sport, the jacket looks great on you. Would you like to take care of it for me for awhile?"

"You mean like baby-sit?" Aaron's eyes shone with eagerness.

Any remnants of E.C.'s previous expression vanished with his laugh. "I guess you could call it that. It's not too cold outside today. We could go to the park and throw the football around if you want," he suggested.

"Sounds like a good idea to me." Anna looked at her brother and winked. "Just let me get something from the kitchen first."

Anna returned holding a plastic bag full of assorted pieces of bread. "We can't forget about the ducks," she said grabbing her own jacket and scarf off the coat rack before leading the three of them out the door in the direction of the park.

"My car is parked over there." E.C. pointed the opposite way.

Anna started to insist on walking but stopped, knowing how special Aaron thought E.C.'s Camaro was. "I guess we could ride this time."

Aaron ran ahead of them to wait by the car.

"Sorry there's not much room in the back seat," E.C. said, letting Aaron climb in and then closing the door for Anna.

Aaron didn't seem to mind. "This is so cool," was his repeated opinion for the entire ride to the park.

"I'll go feed the ducks while you two play catch," Anna said after they got out of the car.

"Are you sure?" E.C. checked.

"I'm sure." Anna watched them for a moment, and then found a spot beside the pond to start tossing bread at the growing number of impatient ducks coming toward her. She thought about what E.C. had gone through. He had every material comfort now that he could want, but Anna knew he would trade it all to have his father and brother back. Louisa wasn't even her own flesh and blood, yet she missed her terribly.

She didn't want to imagine what it would be like if she were to lose her father or Aaron.

"I think you've made some ducks pretty happy."

Anna hadn't heard E.C. walking up to join her. She looked at him first and then at the small amount of bread left in the bag. There were only a few ducks left enjoying the feast around her feet, more than likely the least aggressive of the bunch. The rest of them had gone back into the pond. "I guess I got lost in my thoughts."

"I could see that," he said.

Anna started to laugh when she suddenly became aware that E.C. was alone. Her head swung from side to side. "Where's Aaron?"

E.C. pointed to the playground. "He's playing with a couple of other boys. I didn't think you would mind," E.C. answered calmly.

Anna spotted her brother sliding down a pole and relaxed. "I'm sorry. I try not to overreact. Why don't we wait for him over here?" She walked to the same bench she and Louisa had shared and sat down. It was the same bench E.C. had found her on the day she learned Louisa had died.

She kept her eyes on the pond as she tried to figure out how to begin telling him the truth about Louisa and herself. "Do you know anything about cranes? The birds I mean," she thought to clarify.

E.C.'s face became a picture of bewilderment. "I can't say that I do. I don't think I've ever seen one."

"Louisa told me about them one afternoon while we sat on this same bench watching the ducks. The very full ones now," she added with a smile.

"That's why you were here," he said softly as if to himself.

Anna nodded. "Louisa was from Hungary. She told me about how she and her husband would travel to the lakes so they could watch the cranes as they migrated. Louisa said they would dance as if they were celebrating a grand occasion, but that they simply knew how to celebrate life."

She swallowed hard and looked away from E.C. "She also told me that she and Milo were like the cranes because once they find a mate, they stay together forever. I like to think they're dancing together in heaven along with their son who died in the 1956 revolution."

"So she had a husband and son that died before she did?"

"Yes," Anna answered, realizing too late, the painful similarities between Louisa's past and E.C.'s. She stopped talking, afraid of saying something else that might trigger painful memories for him. They sat together in a long silence.

"Sometimes I wish my mother would have waited to remarry, but not because I don't like Clarence," E.C. finally spoke. "It's just that I hardly had time to adjust to the changes in my first life before I had to begin a new one."

"I'm sure your mother did what she thought was best for both of you." Anna hesitated then asked, "What's your stepfather like?"

E.C. leaned against the back of the bench. "He's a good man, and he runs an honest business. It's him I have to thank for encouraging me to play football."

"I'm sure the team would thank him, too, if they knew," Anna said, turning quiet again while she observed the last remnants of fall color still clinging to the branches. One more strong wind and the remaining leaves would be gone. She had to finish telling E.C. everything before her chance was gone as well. With impulsive resolve she turned and faced him. "I have a lot more I need to tell you."

"Okay," he said, looking surprised.

Anna closed her eyes and drew in a breath of courage before she began. "I've done more than just volunteer at the Samaritan Center. After my father was laid off from Baxter Industries, we didn't have much money until my parents were able to open the café. We were one of those families that ate there, just like the families you've been serving every Wednesday. It could have been me you were spooning out green beans to."

Anna's eyes were locked onto E.C.'s, somehow extracting the strength from them to keep going. "You started volunteering at the center because of Mr. Jenkins' extra credit assignment. I started volunteering because it was the only way I could pay them back for their generosity when my family needed it most. But more than that, it was because I had grown to care about the people there, even Mrs. Harris. For years I blamed your stepfather for making our lives so difficult, but it wasn't until recently that I understood it wasn't his fault."

E.C.'s eyes were pressed together in thought. "I had no idea your father once worked for Baxter Industries. No wonder you were so defensive toward me."

"That wasn't the reason in the beginning. I didn't know Mr. Baxter was your stepfather then." Anna wanted to finish being honest with him. "You were friends with Tonya Sterling, someone I'm not proud to admit I used to be envious of. And you seemed to have it all, the fame, the fortune, the perfect life. Everything I didn't have."

"Perfect, huh?" E.C. I've been envious of something, too. Do you know of what?"

Anna shook her head so that her eyes never left his.

"It's your laugh. From the first time I heard it at Big Jake's and then with Mr. Harmon, I was jealous I wasn't included."

Anna grinned. "I guess that makes us even, though there is one more thing I haven't told you." A breeze blew over them from the pond as Anna paused. "Louisa was much more to me than the housekeeper who lived at the Samaritan Center. Somehow she knew how to teach me play the violin. She's the reason I made All-District and the reason I was going to audition at Truman for a music scholarship." Anna looked down at her hands. "Now everything has changed."

"Not everything has to," E.C. challenged her. "I'm sure she's wondering why you've quit practicing."

"How would you know I wasn't practicing?"

"I'm right, aren't I?"

Anna conceded defeat. "I've tried a few times, but I haven't been able to make the music come alive like it did when Louisa was helping me. The Samaritan Center asked me to play for the Christmas party and I still haven't given them an answer."

"That would be another way for you to give back to them and to honor Louisa for all she did for you." E.C.'s eyebrows were raised in expectation of an answer.

"If I say yes, would you agree to play the piano again?" Anna dared to glimpse at his reaction to her question.

E.C. lowered his head. "Too much time has passed. I think my fingers only know how to hold a football anymore."

"You might be surprised how much your fingers remember," Anna said.

"Maybe," he said giving her a sideways glance. "Speaking of football, I wish the state playoffs weren't out of town."

"You know Aaron and I will be cheering for you, even if we have to from here," Anna said, crossing her arms against the air that had since turned chilly.

E.C. gave Anna a long look. "I'm counting on it. But right now I think I better get you and Aaron home."

"Can I sit in the front seat this time?" Aaron pleaded after they called him away from his new friends.

Anna said no, but that didn't keep him from asking one question after another until Anna let him out in front of the cafe.

"I wish I had his energy," E.C. said.

Anna smiled knowingly. "So do I. Thanks for coming over and taking us to the park," she said and started to get out of the car.

"Anna, wait a minute."

She stopped and turned toward him in the seat.

"I'm glad you told me what you did today."

"So am I."

It seemed E.C. had more he wanted to say making Anna hesitant to leave. But instead of saying something, he leaned in and kissed her forehead. "Can I see you tomorrow?"

Anna barely found enough breath to answer, "Yes."

When she stepped out onto the sidewalk her legs felt so light that they almost buckled beneath her. The weight of her past was gone. E.C. knew everything and he still wanted to see her. Not to mention he kissed her.

It was almost impossible to contain her exhilaration the rest of the evening, especially once Jessie showed up for work. Anna was behind the counter filling drinks when Jessie finally came up and nudged her. "What has gotten into you tonight? I've never seen you quite so....so giddy, not even after you made All-District."

"Giddy?" The word produced unrestrained laughter from Anna.

Jessie lifted her chin in speculation. "Hmm...let me change that to *who* not *what*. And that *who* happens to be named E.C. Coleman."

Anna rolled her eyes. "We're just friends," she said, hoping to cool her best friend's prying instincts.

"Uh-huh...just friends." Jessie's eyes narrowed. "Did you know you have pie on your face?"

A small mirror hung above the soft drink machine and Anna immediately checked her reflection. Jessie was right. Above one eye rested a small bit of meringue from the pie she had sliced earlier. Any other time she would have been humiliated to be seen like that but not tonight. Anna carefully wiped it from her face, and catching Jessie off guard, placed it on hers, laughing, "Now who does..."

Chapter Twenty

Little else but the state playoffs was discussed during Anna's classes at school all the next week. Anna felt the anticipation as well, hoping that Madison would win. As soon as the bell rang on Friday, E.C walked with her out of their government class. Unfortunately, Tonya Sterling was coming toward them from the opposite direction. Ever since All-District they had at least greeted one another, but this time was different. This time she was with E.C., the object of Tonya's unsuccessful conquest.

Anna wondered at Tonya's lack of surprise when her eyes fell on them. She only smiled and poked E.C. as she passed by. "Have you asked her yet?" she asked loud enough for Anna to hear also.

E.C. should have been used to Tonya's brazenness, but when Anna glanced over at him he was visibly flustered and didn't answer. She kept walking, hoping that would put a quick end to the awkward moment.

"Can I give you a ride home?" he said after a few more steps. "I won't get to see you again until after tomorrow's game."

Anna slowed down a little. "I was planning on stopping by the cemetery first. It's been a month since Louisa died."

"I could take you there, unless you'd rather go alone," E.C. offered.

Anna didn't want him to feel obligated in any way. "Only if you're sure you want to?"

"I'm sure," he said.

Once they were in the car, E.C.'s glances kept catching her eye, but otherwise he remained quiet as he drove. Anna knew he was trying to respect her thoughts, however, the one that kept running through her mind wasn't about Louisa or the cemetery; it was about Tonya's question to E.C. in the hallway. Who was the "her" Tonya was referring to?

The question dominated Anna's thinking until E.C. stopped the car on the main road that ran through the middle of the cemetery. Surrounded by row after row of gravesites, her heart was given a harsh reminder of why they were there.

"Do you know which one is Louisa's?" he asked.

"I've only been here once before, but I believe her grave is right over there," Anna said, pointing in the direction of the white cross.

Anna got out of the car and walked to the grave with E.C. close beside her. "I still miss her a lot. I'm sure some people would say I was crazy, but I feel like Louisa knows I'm here. At least I feel better thinking that she does." Anna then pointed to the tombstone next to the cross. "That one is Milo's."

"Why doesn't Louisa have a tombstone like her husband?"

Anna's shoulders rose in uncertainty. "I don't know. I guess she used all their money to buy his. Buying one for herself would have been the last thing on her mind."

E.C. gently turned her to face him. "By the way, I don't think you're crazy."

Anna then watched his eyes shift their focus. A sudden realization made her catch her breath. "Your father and brother are buried here aren't they?"

E.C. motioned with his head, "Beyond that row of trees."

She felt awful as a lump formed in her throat. Of course they would be buried here in the town's main cemetery. "Would you like to walk over there?"

"Another time, maybe," he answered. "Are you ready to leave?"

"Almost, but there's something I need to get first." Anna knelt beside the cross and took a spoon out of her coat pocket.

"What are you doing?" Concern filled E.C.'s words.

Anna swung her chin up to look at him. "It's okay, you'll understand in a minute." She then proceeded to dig a hole in the ground next to the cross.

She didn't have to dig very far before reaching the medal she had buried on her previous visit. Anna brushed as much of the dirt away as possible, though the attached ribbon was now stained with mud.

"At first I thought Louisa deserved to have my All-District medal more than me. But then I decided I should keep it as a reminder of the special gift she gave to me. She helped me to believe in myself." Anna closed it in her hand and stood up. "Now, I'm ready."

E.C. was just as quiet in the car on the return trip home. He cleared his throat a couple times, making Anna think he intended to speak, but nothing was ever said.

When he cleared his throat a third time, Anna felt compelled to ask him, "Are you all right?"

By then they were almost at the café. E.C. pulled over to the curb a few feet back from the front door. "I've been trying to ask you something."

Anna pretended she didn't notice his inability to maintain eye contact with her and waited patiently. "The winter formal is coming up and I wanted to know if you would go with me," he finally asked before turning toward her for an answer.

Anna's heart pounded noticeably in her chest while she thought back to the moment in the hallway when Tonya poked E.C.. "So that's what Tonya's question was about?"

E.C. nodded. "I don't think she knows what it means to be subtle."

Anna struggled to make sense of the situation. "You mean Tonya knew you were going to ask me?"

"She insisted it was time I had a date, and that if I didn't find one myself, she was going to find one for me. It just so happens we were both thinking of the same person." E.C. smiled at her. "For whatever reason, I think she feels as if she needs to put up a front. Underneath it all, though, she does like you."

Remembering, the weekend they shared at All-District, Anna knew E.C.'s observation was correct. She had witnessed Tonya's attempts at projecting unrealistic perfection firsthand. Anna could only guess that Tonya had given up on being his girlfriend. "Who is Tonya going with?"

He laughed. "Can you believe, Taylor?"

E.C. seemed to be more relaxed, but Anna wasn't. Old insecurities were resurfacing to declare mutiny on her new feelings of trust.

"You still haven't given me an answer. Anna, would you go to the Christmas formal with me?" he asked again, this time with more confidence.

Anna tried to stall, unable to tell which side of her internal battle was winning. "When is it?"

"December 11th," he answered.

If Anna had needed an excuse, she now had one. The truth was she wanted to go. "That's the same night of the Christmas party at the Samaritan Center."

E.C.'s head lowered then lifted with a discouraged smile. "My first attempt at a date and I get turned down."

The initial rush of excitement Anna felt at being asked was gone "I'm sorry. You know I have to be there."

Heartstrings

E.C. gave her a look of resignation. "I know, especially because they've asked you to play your violin, and that's something you need to do."

Anna wanted to tell him that if he thought she needed to play the violin then it was only fair that he play the piano again. If she wasn't able to change his mind, she knew there was only one other person that could.

E.C. glanced at his watch. "I guess I better get going. We have a team meeting back at the school."

Anna reached into the front pocket of her jeans. "Here," she said, placing a penny in his hand. "I haven't made a wish on it yet. Maybe it will bring you good luck."

E.C. rolled the penny between his thumb and his finger before putting it in his glove box. "I'm counting on it," he said thoughtfully with an added wink.

Anna watched as he drove off in the direction of the school, knowing what she had to do next. After telling her mother she was taking a walk, Anna set out for her favorite street.

Once she reached her destination, an ambush of palpitations raced through her body. Anna's eyes slowly traced the perimeter of the Baxter Mansion, marking the stone and wrought iron home she had admired for years. She never thought she would ever be approaching its front door, hoping to enter. Yet, here she stood fighting the temptation to turn around and run. She trembled with nerves at what Mrs. Baxter's reaction would be.

Anna placed her finger over the doorbell button. "It's now or never," she whispered before applying enough pressure to make it ring.

Her mouth was poised to greet Mrs. Baxter until the door swung open and she realized that another woman was peering at her instead.

"May I help you?"

The woman's stature and white hair bore an uncanny resemblance to Louisa causing Anna to pull back and collect her bearings. "I…I was hoping to find Mrs. Baxter at home, but I can come back another time."

"If you would care to step inside and wait a moment, I'll tell her you are here. Who may I say is visiting?" the woman asked.

"Anna Holmes, please." Anna wanted to abandon her mission, but her feet were already moving her body forward through the doorway.

Her fingers fidgeted inside her coat pockets while the door closed behind her and she was left alone in the entryway. The reality of being inside the walls of this home filled her with awe and impending fear. Would she be able to speak? Would Mrs. Baxter even remember her? Anna wouldn't allow her eyes to wander as much as they wanted to, but what she did see was grander than she had imagined. The chandelier suspended from the tall ceiling caught her attention first. Its hundreds of glass prisms sparkled, projecting a glittery pattern of light on the wall.

"Hello, Anna."

Anna turned her face toward Mrs. Baxter and looked again into E.C.'s mother's eyes. They were the same eyes she noted at the café, only this time Anna knew she had been married to Charlie Coleman, a bookstore owner, and had lost both a husband and a son.

"Hi, Mrs. Baxter, I hope you don't mind me being here."

"Of course not, please come and sit down."

Anna followed Mrs. Baxter into a small sitting room adjacent to the entryway, her mind absorbing the arrangement of its furnishings. There were two brocade chairs in deep red, separated by a carved mahogany table, and two barrister style bookcases completely filled with books. The room's focus, however, was undeniably on the grand piano that sat diagonal in the far corner of the room. Anna sat down in one of the chairs but her eyes remained fixed on the ebony colored instrument. Its lacquered surface shone with distinction, though the keys were covered and there was no evidence of music anywhere. The piano gave the impression of a fine piece of furniture, yet she saw it as nothing more than a coffin for lost memories.

"What can I do for you, Anna?" Mrs. Baxter spoke from the other chair.

Anna took strength from the piano's presence to speak. "I came because I was hoping you could do something for E.C. ...or I mean, Evan."

Mrs. Baxter looked questioningly at Anna. "What is it you are hoping I can do?"

Anna knew she couldn't hesitate or she would lose her nerve. "I thought you could encourage him to play the piano again. He's been afraid to ever since his father died."

"Afraid?"

"That hearing the piano would bring back too many painful memories for you."

Anna diverted her eyes knowing they wouldn't have to peer very deeply into Mrs. Baxter's to discover the grief still present in them.

Mrs. Baxter's voice became faint. "We never talk about the past."

"I think Evan wants to. He wants to know his father and brother haven't been forgotten."

Mrs. Baxter's eyes closed and when they opened again Anna witnessed a profound sadness. "Those were such difficult times, and our lives are so different now."

Anna was sitting close enough to Mrs. Baxter to reach out and touch her hand. "I'm sorry, Mrs. Baxter, I never meant to upset you. It's just that I've learned the past will always be a part of who we are. Happy or sad, it can't be boxed up and put away in an attic."

Mrs. Baxter looked at Anna but said nothing in response.

Anna stood up and walked over to touch the lid to the piano. "Evan told me his father taught him how to play, but without your blessing that music may stay gone from his life forever."

She started to leave then stopped. "I also wanted to let you know the Samaritan Center's Christmas party is coming up soon, and I thought you and Mr. Baxter might like to come." She tried to add a small smile. "Our café will be providing the dessert, so there should be plenty of butterscotch pie."

After letting herself out of the house, Anna didn't stop moving until she reached the next block. It was then that she felt the quivering in her legs accompanied by a hard knot in her stomach. She hadn't planned on saying what she did; the words seemed to form in her mouth and speak by their own will.

Of the many things she learned from Louisa, one was that great things weren't accomplished without some risk. If E.C's and his mother's memories continued to stay locked behind walls of silence, it wouldn't be because she didn't try to find the key.

Chapter Twenty-One

Anna was apprehensive when she saw E.C. after the game. Not only had Madison lost the playoffs, she also didn't know whether his mother had told him about her visit. If she had, he didn't say anything. Nor did he seem near as disappointed about the loss as she expected. He had been more concerned about how Taylor felt, since it was his fumble that set up the winning touchdown for the opposing team.

With the football season over, conversations at school shifted to the upcoming formal. Anna had never cared about attending a dance before, yet the more she listened to others talk about it, the more she found herself secretly yearning to attend. It was too late though. She had already told E.C. she couldn't go, and there was still the Samaritan Center party to help with.

When the night of the formal arrived, there was nothing Anna could do but dream about what she was missing. She left the café and walked the familiar route to the Samaritan Center. It was just as well she wasn't going, since that would have meant asking her parents to buy a dress, something they may not have been able to afford.

The wind was cold, and an extra strong gust whipped Anna's cheeks as she fought to turn the knob on the front door of the center. "It's probably as frozen as I am," she groaned, though hating to complain too loudly. This party was the highlight of the year for the people that came there.

Anna set her violin on the ground to free both hands when the door suddenly opened.

"I thought I heard someone rattling the door to get in. Come on in and join us," Mr. Harmon said in his usual jovial manner.

"Thanks, Mr. Harmon." She stepped inside and began removing her coat. "Who else is already here?"

"Someone like you who wants to practice before the party," he answered with a grin.

Anna thought hard to remember the plans that had been discussed. "I didn't realize there was other entertainment." She quickly dismissed the idea that maybe she could have gone to the dance after all.

As she hung up her scarf and hat she heard music emanating from what sounded like a piano. Anna walked around the corner and stopped. She couldn't believe what she was seeing. Placed in the corner was a small console piano with E.C. sitting on its bench. His eyes shone with satisfaction as if he had pulled off the biggest coup in history.

Anna's mouth dropped to speak but nothing came out.

"The piano and I are both a little rusty, but as long as you don't mind, we'll try not to mess you up," E.C. said, breaking into a smile.

Anna finally found her voice. "I don't understand. Where did the piano come from?"

"My mother knew someone who needed to find a new home for it and thought the Samaritan Center would be a good place."

"And you're going to play it with me?"

"I brought my book of Christmas songs my father gave me, but I won't play if you don't want me to." E.C.'s expression became uncertain.

"No,...no, I want you to." Anna hurried to refute any doubts he might be having and returned a smile. "I'm glad you're here. But I may be the one messing you up. You know I haven't been practicing much lately," she added more solemnly as her thoughts drifted to Louisa.

E.C. got up and placed himself in front of Anna. He held her arms, refocusing her attention on him. "It's time for that to change. The only one who has had trouble believing in you is yourself."

The intensity of his words bore through her, and she could no longer look him in the eye. What he said was true. The confidence she gained making All-District had since been buried with Louisa.

"Anna, you can accomplish whatever you decide to. You have more courage than anyone I know when it comes to doing the right thing," he continued.

The strong undercurrent in his voice suggested to Anna that he knew about her visit with his mother.

How else would both a piano and E.C. have ended up at the party. She was thankful she had made a difference between E.C. and his mother, but for now she had to ignore his statement. "I guess we better start practicing before everyone gets here."

Anna could have replied that having courage wasn't enough. That without another letter of recommendation and more lessons there wasn't any hope of getting a scholarship to Truman. But she pulled her violin out of its case instead and did her best to tune with the slightly off key piano. "Shall we start with 'Deck the Halls'?" she finally suggested.

E.C.'s hands glided naturally across the keys, belying the fact that he hadn't touched a piano in many years. Anna shoved aside her self-conscious inhibitions and began playing with him. Within a few measures, she was touched by a palpable awareness of how much she missed playing her violin in the way Louisa had taught her. It was as if Louisa's energy was trying to beat life back into her heart and her fingers.

They played continuously while people arrived and ate their dinner. The beginning of each new song brought increasing appreciation from the growing number of guests, with some of them even starting to sing along. Each time the door opened Anna looked over, hoping to see that Mrs. Baxter had accepted her invitation. Her eyes also checked the dessert table to make sure there was plenty of pie left if she did come.

Anna saw her mother tap her finger on her watch to signal that it was almost time for the gifts to be passed out to the children. She turned to E.C.. "Why don't we end with, 'We Wish You a Merry Christmas'."

With the last word of the song, a surprising and boisterous, "Ho, Ho, Ho, Merry Christmas!" boomed from the hallway.

Anna expected to see Santa Claus come through the doorway, but this one surprised her. He looked so much more authentic compared to those the center had dressed in the past. The children jumped out of their seats with excitement.

"Have all you boys and girls been good?" Santa asked.

A loud, "Yes," sounded in unison.

"Then how about a toy and special book for each one of you," Santa continued.

E.C. was standing beside Anna when Mrs. Baxter wheeled in a cart stacked with children's books. Anna turned to E.C. to see his reaction.

His face wore no expression as he stared at the scene in front of him. "Those are books from the attic…from my father's bookstore," he said slowly, "…and that man playing Santa is my stepfather."

Anna had no previous conception of what Mr. Baxter looked like in his real person but he made a very believable Santa Claus. "Shh, don't let anyone know," she whispered back.

Mrs. Baxter caught E.C.'s stare and started walking toward them. Anna wanted to disappear, still insecure that she had interfered too much, but it was too late.

"I know how happy your father would be that these books came to the Samaritan Center, and I also know how proud he would be of you." She then looked at Anna, "Of both of you."

Anna saw her parents coming to join them led by her mother. "Thank you, Mrs. Baxter, for helping to make this such a special Christmas party," Mrs. Holmes said.

"Please, call me Mona, and I should be thanking you. This is the best Christmas I've had in a long time," she said, throwing a smile at Anna and E.C., "made even better with those delicious pies."

Anna looked over to the table where the pies had been and saw that it was almost empty. For the first time she understood the pride her father felt in owning the café.

"Anna." Mr. Deacon approached their small group, and held out an envelope to her. "We found this when we were going through Louisa's belongings."

Anna looked at Mr. Deacon and then at the envelope. She lifted it from his hand as if it was a fragile piece of crystal, unable to take her eyes off of the scribbling of letters spelling her name on the front. Her fingers began to tremble as she opened the flap. The piece of paper she pulled out was the recommendation form for Truman filled out in the same handwriting. Anna was overwhelmed; humbled by Louisa's completion of a task she knew must have been difficult for her.

As Anna's eyes continued to scroll down the paper, they came to rest on Louisa's signature. There was her name, Louisa Kovack, which Anna immediately recognized, but there was more written beside it. She looked at the words more closely, deciphering each one out loud, "Hungarian State Symphony Orchestra, 1949-1956."

"Louisa never told me," she said softly as the knowledge of Louisa's past became more obvious. "Of course she knew how to play the violin."

"I assume that's why she kept this," Mr. Deacon interrupted.

Anna looked at him in question, and then at the violin case he lifted up to her.

"There's a note inside," he said, handing it to her.

She hesitated, looking at the faces of everyone around her.

"You should open it, Anna," Mrs. Baxter urged her.

Anna took the case and set it carefully on the piano bench. By now her entire hand was shaking, but she managed to unhook the latch and pull up the top half of the case. The vision before her was blurred by moisture, but Anna knew what was inside. She carefully picked up the violin, admiring its rich red-brown color and well preserved condition as she did. Anna then handed the note to E.C.. "Will you read this for me?"

E.C. took in a breath before starting. "My dearest Anna, My heart bursts with pride when I think how far you have come. Only you can make this instrument sing again. Just remember the cranes, and remember always to dance with joy. All my love, Louisa.

Anna shook her head fighting to maintain her composure. "I don't know how I can without a teacher, and I don't have one anymore."

"I know of a very fine violin player. He was a good friend of Charlie's," Mrs. Baxter said.

"Thank you, Mrs. Baxter, but we can't possibly…"

"Yes we can, Anna," her father spoke up with an affirming nod from her mother.

Anna was quiet as the tears could no longer be contained. "I don't know what to say. I feel like this is all a dream, that I'm going to wake up and none of this will have happened."

"Well, the dream's not over yet," a familiar voice boomed in.

Anna jerked her head around. "Jessie! How long have you been here?"

Jessie came up beside Anna and touched the violin before answering, "Long enough to know that you deserve everything that is good."

Anna wiped her eyes to get a better look at her best friend and noticed something draped over her arm. "What is that?" she asked.

Jessie glanced at her watch. "It's only 8:30. There's still time to make it to the winter formal. Besides, this dress from my aunt's wedding is just itching to be worn again."

Anna saw Jessie wink at E.C. and looked toward him for an explanation.

"I know you said you couldn't go because of this party, but I was hoping with Jessie's help you would reconsider. "I'm asking you again. Anna Holmes, will you go to the dance with me?"

"I...," she started, touching the salty, wet stains on her face.

"The answer is 'yes'," Jessie said as she took hold of Anna's arm and pulled her away. "She'll be ready in just a few minutes."

"Jessie, I've never done anything like this before," Anna protested once they were inside the office and the door was closed.

"That's exactly why you should go, not to mention that there's one very nice, very handsome E.C. Coleman out there waiting for you. Remember ...adventures dared...," Jessie said.

"But you and Kyle were supposed to be going to this formal. It's not fair."

Jessie began brushing Anna's hair up and placing hairpins in it to hold the curls. "The flu isn't known for its fairness. I'm just glad I could help E.C. devise this plan."

"I don't think I even know how to dance," Anna pleaded as Jessie stood back to look at her work.

"Trust me, you'll be fine. Now let's get these shoes and dress on," Jessie commanded.

The royal blue satin slipped easily over Anna's frame, draping fluidly down the back. Other than Jessie being a little taller, they were close enough in size that the dress fit perfectly.

"Now let me see you." Jessie shook her head with approval. "Anna Holmes, you are a picture of beauty, inside and out."

Jessie held up her pinky finger. "Promise me you'll have a great time."

Anna linked her pinky finger with Jessie's, and then slowly opened the door. Her eyes widened when she saw that E.C. had changed into a dark suit and was standing in front of her holding a corsage. This moment was real. For the first time in her life, she was going to a dance.

After her mother helped to pin the corsage on, E.C. offered Anna his arm. "Shall we?"

Before they reached the door, Aaron stepped in front of them. He didn't say anything, but looked first at Anna and then at E.C., finally holding up his hand to give E.C. a high five. Everyone laughed then began clapping as they continued out of the building.

"I hope it was okay that I asked Jessie for her assistance. I wasn't sure you would go, otherwise," E.C. said once they were inside the car, "though maybe this had something to do with it." He opened his hand to reveal the penny Anna had given him before the state playoff game.

All Anna could think about was Madison losing. "I'm sorry it didn't end up bringing you good luck."

E.C. looked hard into her eyes forcing her to focus on his long eyelashes. "But it did. I didn't use my wish for the game; I saved it for tonight hoping I could still take you to the dance."

Anna was stunned. "Really?"

"Really," he smiled.

"I guess we owe a special thanks to Jessie and the lucky penny then." She smiled back then folded her arms to prevent any further cold air from wrapping around her bare shoulders.

"Here, put my coat on. You're going to need it where we're going first anyway, as long as you don't mind taking a little detour," E.C. said.

"I don't mind." Anna's eyes kept watch as she followed the direction in which he drove.

When he turned through the gate into the cemetery, she felt an unexpected shiver, though not from the cold or from the fact that they were in a cemetery after dark. Maybe it was because she felt like Louisa had been with her, watching over her all evening.

"I was going to show you something tomorrow, but after what happened tonight I couldn't wait any longer." E.C. stopped the car and got out, then helped Anna. "There should be enough light to see it."

She couldn't imagine what he was talking about. There was only one reason for her to be at this cemetery and he appeared to be in a hurry to get there. E.C. took her hand. "Close your eyes until I tell you to open them."

Anna looked into the face she had grown to trust. "Promise not to let go."

E.C. tightened his grip. "I promise."

He led her the short distance to their destination. "You can open them now."

Anna let out a small gasp. There was no longer a small narrow cross on Louisa's grave. It had been replaced by a tombstone the same size as Milo's. The light from the tall lamps and almost full moon allowed

Anna to make out the letters that spelled her name. But there was something else engraved and barely visible that prompted Anna to move in closer to get a better look.

"It's a crane with its wings spread open. After what you told me about them, I thought it was appropriate," he said.

Anna dared to touch the engraving before turning to E.C.. "It's perfect…but how?"

"I asked Clarence if Baxter Industries would be willing to provide one since she had worked at the Samaritan Center, but also because of how much she meant to you."

Anna threw her arms around his neck and hugged him. There wasn't another place she felt warmer and more secure. "Thank you," she whispered.

Neither one seemed in a hurry to loosen their hold. But when they did, their lips drew together for their first real kiss, tender and honest. As right and natural as it felt, Anna finally pulled back. "Come on, we better get to the dance so we can make Louisa proud."

They were walking back toward the car when Anna suddenly felt a strange urge to glance over her shoulder.

"Is something wrong?" E.C. asked.

Anna laughed as she envisioned herself having wings. "Oh, it's nothing. It's just that tonight…I feel like I could fly."

A Note from the Author

"October 23, 1956, is a day that will live forever in the annals of free men and nations. It was a day of courage, conscience and triumph. No other day since history began has shown more clearly the eternal unquenchability of man's desire to be free, whatever the odds against success, whatever the sacrifice required."

-John F. Kennedy, on the first anniversary of the Hungarian Revolution

On October 23, 1956, thousands of protestors took to the streets of Budapest, Hungary to rise up against Soviet rule, demanding a more democratic political system in their country. By that evening, what began as a peaceful demonstration escalated into a full-scale riot when the police opened fire on the crowd. A revolution had begun.

For a short time it looked as if the Hungarians were succeeding and peace might be restored. Then on November 4, 1956, Soviet forces rolled into Budapest with heavy artillery and launched a major attack, crushing once and for all the national uprising started twelve days earlier.

The defeat of the Hungarian revolution was one of the darkest moments of the Cold War. Over 200,000 Hungarians fled across the border into Austria and the West until that route was sealed off, while many that remained were arrested, imprisoned or executed. Though fictional characters, Louisa and Milo represent those Hungarians who were lucky enough to escape. And like similar families throughout history, their son, Felix, paid the ultimate sacrifice for his country. He died for freedom.

If you enjoyed *Heartstrings*,
Watch for *Becoming Rose*
coming in 2016

Becoming Rose

Leopold held his breath as he slipped through the

shadows of darkness

His once beloved country was a stranger to him now

He had no other choice but to escape…or die

Petrograd, Russia, 1917…

Acknowledgments

I hardly know how to begin saying thank you to all those who made this book possible, but what better place than at the beginning...

To my mother who never got to read this book. Her spirit of belief that I could accomplish whatever I set my mind on carried me through its completion. She lived a life of selflessness and steadfast faith, and I am forever grateful to have been her daughter.

To my family, I love you every minute of every day. You make me smile and inspire me to do my very best in all I do.

To Wordweavers, who from the first time I stepped into a meeting made me feel that was where I belonged. I am lucky to be part of this supportive community of friends and writers.

To David Carrico and Larry Nix, whose honesty and guidance helped me persevere though the first draft of this novel.

To Heather Davis, Christine Jarmola, and Jennifer McMurrain, whose constant doses of laughter and encouragement keep me writing and whose invaluable insight helped shape the final draft.

To Brandy Walker, whose talent and vision created the amazing cover and brought this story to life for me.

To all of you, a heart full of thanks. I couldn't have done it without you.

About the Author

Marilyn Boone is a former elementary school teacher, having taught grades first through fifth. When not writing, she enjoys many other creative and musical activities, including learning how to play her hammered dulcimer.

Heartstrings, was a previous award winning book at the Oklahoma Writer's Federation Inc. annual conference and contest. It is the first Legacy Novel, young adult inspirational books containing a little history, a little mystery, and always a little romance. Watch for the next book, *Becoming Rose*, to be released soon.

Other works by
Marilyn Boone

Book Contributor
Chicken Soup of the Soul: Reboot Your Life

Collaborative Novel
A Weekend with Effie

Anthologies
Seasons Remembered
Seasons of Life

Visit her on her website
http://www.marilynboone.com